F Meacham, L.

ACCLAIM FOR THE NOVELS OF
LEILA MEACHAM

TITANS

"The novel has it all: a wide cast of characters, pitch-perfect period detail, romance, plenty of drama, and skeletons in the closet (literally). Saga fans will be swooning."

—*Booklist* (starred review)

"It has everything any reader could want in a book...epic story-telling that plunges the reader headfirst into the plot... [Meacham] is a titan herself."

—Huffington Post

"Emotionally resounding...Texas has never seemed grander... Meacham's easy-to-read prose helps to maintain a pace that you won't be able to quit, pushing through from chapter to chapter to find the next important nugget of this dramatic family tale. It is best savored over a great steak with a glass of wine and evenings to yourself."

—BookReporter

SOMERSET

"Bestselling author Meacham is back with a prequel to *Roses* that stands on its own as a sweeping historical saga, spanning the nineteenth century...[Fans] and new readers alike will find themselves absorbed in the family saga that Meacham has proven—once again—talented in telling."

—*Publishers Weekly* (starred review)

"Entertaining…Meacham skillfully weaves colorful history into her lively tale…*Somerset* has its charms."

—*Dallas Morning News*

"Slavery, westward expansion, abolition, the Civil War, love, marriage, friendship, tragedy, and triumph—all the ingredients (and much more) that made so many love *Roses* so much—are here in abundance."

—*San Antonio Express-News*

"A story you do not want to miss…[Recommended] to readers of Kathryn Stockett's *The Help* or Margaret Mitchell's *Gone with the Wind*. *Somerset* has everything a compelling historical epic calls for: love and war, friendship and betrayal, opportunity and loss, and everything in between."

—*BookPage*

"4½ stars! This prequel to *Roses* is as addictive as any soap opera…As sprawling and big as Texas itself, Meacham's epic saga is perfect for readers who long for the 'big books' of the past. There are enough adventure, tears, and laughter alongside colorful history to keep readers engrossed and satisfied."

—*RT Book Reviews*

TUMBLEWEEDS

"[An] expansive generational saga…Fans of *Friday Night Lights* will enjoy a return to the land where high school football boys are kings."

—*Chicago Tribune*

"Meacham scores a touchdown... You will laugh, cry, and cheer to a plot so thick and a conclusion so surprising, it will leave you wishing for more. Yes, Meacham is really that good. And *Tumbleweeds* is more than entertaining, it's addictive."

—Examiner.com

"If you're going to a beach this summer, or better yet, a windswept prairie, this is definitely a book you'll want to pack."
—*Wilkes-Barre Times Leader* (PA)

"[A] sprawling novel as large as Texas itself."

—*Library Journal*

"Once again, Meacham has proven to be a master storyteller... The pages fly by as the reader becomes engrossed in the tale."

—*Lubbock-Avalanche Journal* (TX)

ROSES

"Like *Gone with the Wind*, as gloriously entertaining as it is vast... *Roses* transports."

—*People*

"Meacham's sweeping, century-encompassing, multigenerational epic is reminiscent of the film *Giant*, and as large, romantic, and American a tale as Texas itself."

—*Booklist*

"Enthralling."

—*Better Homes and Gardens*

"The story of East Texas families in the kind of dynastic gymnastics we all know and love."

—Liz Smith

"Larger-than-life protagonists and a fast-paced, engaging plot…Meacham has succeeded in creating an indelible heroine."

—*Dallas Morning News*

"[An] enthralling stunner, a good, old-fashioned read."

—*Publishers Weekly*

"A thrilling journey…a treasure…a must-read. Warning: Once you begin reading, you won't be able to put the book down."

—Examiner.com

"[A] sprawling novel of passion and revenge. Highly recommended…It's been almost thirty years since the heyday of giant epics in the grand tradition of Edna Ferber and Barbara Taylor Bradford, but Meacham's debut might bring them back."

—*Library Journal* (starred review)

"A high-end *Thorn Birds*."

—TheDailyBeast.com

"I ate this multigenerational tale of two families warring it up across Texas history with the same alacrity with which I would gobble chocolate."

—Joshilyn Jackson, *New York Times* bestselling author of *gods in Alabama* and *Backseat Saints*

"A Southern epic in the most cinematic sense—plot-heavy and historical, filled with archaic Southern dialect and formality, with love, marriage, war, and death over three generations."

—Caroline Dworin, "The Book Bench," NewYorker.com

"This sweeping epic of love, sacrifice, and struggle reads like *Gone with the Wind* with all the passions and family politics of the South."

—*Midwest Book Review*

"The kind of book you can lose yourself in, from beginning to end."

—Huffington Post

"Fast-paced and full of passions…This panoramic drama proves evocative and lush. The plot is intricate and gives back as much as the reader can take…Stunning and original, *Roses* is a must-read."

—TheReviewBroads.com

"May herald the overdue return of those delicious doorstop epics from such writers as Barbara Taylor Bradford and Colleen McCullough…a refreshingly nostalgic bouquet of family angst, undying love, and 'if only's."

—*Publishers Weekly*

"Superbly written…a rating of ten out of ten. I simply loved this book."

—ANovelMenagerie.com

ALY'S HOUSE

Leila Meacham

GRAND CENTRAL
PUBLISHING

NEW YORK   BOSTON

Grand Central Publishing
Hachette Book Group
1290 Avenue of the Americas
New York, NY 10104
grandcentralpublishing.com
twitter.com/grandcentralpub

Originally published in hardcover in 1985 by the Walker Publishing Company, Inc., New York, New York.

First Grand Central Publishing Edition: October 2016

Grand Central Publishing is a division of Hachette Book Group, Inc.
The Grand Central Publishing name and logo is a trademark of Hachette Book Group, Inc.

The publisher is not responsible for websites (or their content) that are not owned by the publisher.

The Hachette Speakers Bureau provides a wide range of authors for speaking events. To find out more, go to www.hachettespeakersbureau.com or call (866) 376-6591.

PCCN: 2016941669

ISBNs: 978-1-4555-4137-9 (trade pbk.), 978-1-4555-4136-2 (library edition hardcover), 978-1-4555-4134-8 (ebook)

Printed in the United States of America

LSC-C

10 9 8 7 6 5 4 3 2 1

To my niece Jeri,
who sees for all of us.

A Letter to My Friends, Fans, Readers of My Later-In-Life Novels and Newcomers to the Books of Leila Meacham

Dear Ones,

Aly's House *is another in the series of three romance novels I wrote in the mid-eighties. For those of you who are famil-iar with my much later novels only*—Roses, Tumbleweeds, Somerset, *and* Titans—*you'll no doubt notice the differ-ence in the physical size and narrative scope and writing quality of this book. Pray, don't be too harsh in your judg-ment.* Aly's House *represents one of my first sorties into the field of fiction writing and was written under the coer-cion of a contract to the publisher of my first romance novel to produce another. There is no pain like the obligation to create a work of fiction with a plot, cast of characters, set-ting, beginning, middle, and end, and give it a* title *when you have no idea of the who, the what, the where, and the when, and all under the whip of a deadline. Thus it was with* Aly's House. *"Write what you know" is the mantra creative-writing teachers tell their students and authors of books on "how to write a bestseller" instruct their readers, and for many writers that works. The elements of the novel are all in place, and they make a fine career writing about what they know. Well, that's all fine and dandy if you know anything of interest to fill nearly two hundred pages of a ro-*

mance novel or have the nerve to write about persons of your acquaintance. I had neither knowledge nor nerve.

So I decided to write about what I didn't know. That entailed creating people on paper I had never known, living lives I had never experienced, in places I had never been. Where to start? In one's curiosity was as good a place as any. I had always been curious about and admiring of horses, not that I'd ever ridden or owned one. I simply thought them magnificent animals. I would begin there, within the strong human desire to learn more about a subject. Memory was another place to explore. Surely in the power of the mind to remember was stuck an indelible image, a fleeting but memorable moment, a phrase never forgotten that could trigger an idea, a character, a conflict. And then into focus came the remembrance of a farmhouse I had seen briefly from the window of a school bus returning with my students from a field trip. From its windows wafted the most heavenly supper smells that reached my nostrils as we drove by. Lights were on in the kitchen, and I could see several children bent over their homework at the table, a mother at the stove. A happy family lives there, I remember thinking at the time.

Horses and farmhouses—I could work with that. And so out of my curiosity, Sampson was born, and from a brief glimpse fixed in memory, the house on Cedar Hill came into being. From there it was a matter of fleshing out from research, interviews, up-close-and-personal chats with horses, and imagination. A writer does not always have to have experienced to create. After completing Aly's House, *I retired my faithful old electric Smith-Corona from writing fiction to return to teaching and did not sit down before another typing machine to once again try my hand at composing a novel until twenty-five years later—this time to a Hewlett-Packard home computer. I was too old then, or wise, I'd like to believe, to worry about the outcome of my efforts. What would be, would be. It's turned out to be a great return trip.*

I leave you with this scene from Aly's House *in which Aly, the young daughter of a wealthy banker, recollects saying to Elizabeth, the wife of a poor farmer in her modest home on Cedar Hill:*

"You live…very grandly here."

"Grandly?" Elizabeth had puzzled over the words, thinking no doubt of the splendid house where Aly lived, and wondered at the child's meaning. "No, not grandly, child, but we live very happily here."

"Isn't that living grandly?" Aly had wanted to know.

And so I wish the same for you. Live grandly.

Leila Meacham

ALY'S HOUSE

Chapter One

With a sigh, Aly Kingston laid aside the newspaper she had bought to read while waiting for her flight to Oklahoma City. Texas newspapers, like those in her own home state, were filled these days with little but the woes brought on by the oil glut. Every other story seemed devoted to a small town, bank, or school district struggling to survive without the revenue of a once high-riding industry caught in a slump. She didn't have to read about them. In Claiborne, she saw evidence of all three daily.

How fast the house of cards had fallen once the demand for oil decreased, leaving everybody but a fortunate few caught in the collapse. She had been among the fortunate few. Her business had not been founded on the vagaries of oil production, but on the breeding of quality horses and purse-winning racing stock. So far she'd suffered only the enviable problem of trying to keep up with the demand.

She had just about decided to browse in the gift shop when a tall man—dark, slim, impossibly handsome—strode into her vision from the concourse. She sat transfixed, disbelieving, her heart nearly failing at the sight of the familiar figure headed for a panel of telephones directly in front of her.

It was Marshall Wayne. There was not the slightest doubt

that it was he. Time had not changed him, merely polished and refined, strengthened and enhanced his figure—just as she had known it would. She would have known him anywhere, at any age. A whole gallery of his portraits, sketched mentally each year, still hung in her heart.

He had not seen her. She looked hurriedly around for the newspaper to shield her face until she could adjust to the shock of seeing him again. A man one seat over had picked it up, and she decided against asking for it back to avoid calling attention to herself. Opening her purse, she took out her ticket—anything to read, to focus on—while her heart stilled and her vision cleared. Marshall had lifted the receiver and was dialing.

What was the matter with her? How could she react this way? Here she was, almost past thirty, successful, admired, and respected, yet still at the mercy of some paralyzing infatuation with a man she suspected wouldn't spit on her if she were on fire—even after thirteen years.

His back was to her. She looked up from the ticket surreptitiously, hurriedly taking in the long, lithe form she remembered—the shape of the dark head, the set of the shoulders. His suit was impeccable, superbly tailored and rich in quality. So time had brought it all, had it—the money and importance he had so craved? She was glad, though not surprised. For people like Marshall Wayne, blessed with such intelligence and looks, success was a plum waiting to be picked.

So in the few minutes before she caught her plane, why didn't she simply get up and walk over to him, present herself? Prosperity and time had probably long assuaged the sting of the old injuries and animosities, just as her father had predicted. Other than an occasional unpleasant memory of them, Marshall probably never thought of the Kingstons at all anymore, certainly not of her. For her own sake, she would so like to put some sort of an end to this—this unfinished business between them. She thought of it as an essential page ripped out of a book. All these years she had wanted to put it to rights, restore it, smooth it out so that she could close the book. Just a few minutes to explain was all she needed. Then he could be on his way and she hers, their chapter finished, done.

She would have to tell him who she was. He would not recognize her now. Even she sometimes had trouble recognizing the rather stunning, fashionable woman in her mirror, the woman she sometimes thought of as "Emmalou Fuller."

So why didn't she just get up and do that once he'd finished his phone call?

Suddenly, as if someone had called his name, Marshall turned to her, the receiver cradled in his shoulder while he fished for something in the breast pocket of his coat. Their glances struck, fused, and held for several rapt seconds before Aly lowered hers in embarrassment, burning with an adolescent blush that crept slowly over her face through the roots of her hair. Good God! She might just as well still be in grade school, still be sitting at his mother's table when he walked in the kitchen door.

Say hello to Aly, son.

The ticket blurred with the poignancy of the memory, of the sudden vivid recollection of those long-ago afternoons and the sound of Elizabeth Wayne's voice, silent over a decade now.

Aly remembered the first time she had heard that beloved voice, one winter afternoon when she and Willy had stopped by Cedar Hill on the way home from school. Willy had taken the basket of clean wash into the farmhouse and returned with the faultlessly ironed pieces; and she had helped him hang the shirts and carefully stack the folded things in the back of the big car. Then the Cadillac had refused to start. Elizabeth had come out onto the porch in her print housedress and apron and called to Willy, bent over the motor with her husband, "Do you think the little girl might like to come inside the house? She's probably cold out there."

Willy, the family's chauffeur and handyman, had extricated himself from beneath the hood and inquired of the freckled face staring out the backseat window, "You want to go inside, Punkin?"

"Sure," she said, scrambling out with her science book, her cold toes throbbing in her loafers.

"If that's homework, you're welcome to sit here at the table and work on it," Elizabeth Wayne invited as they entered the warm, fragrant kitchen. It smelled of apples baking and clean laundry. "Hungry? How about a glass of milk and a piece of apple pie?"

Aly had nodded and sat down at the oilcloth-covered table partly piled with stacks of folded laundry. Soon a large slice of flaky pie and a glass of milk were set before her. Her stomach began to clamor. Slowly, her eyes on the pie, she removed her coat while Elizabeth went back to her ironing. Aly rarely ate anything. She didn't care for the food at home, and the cafeteria lunches at school were even more unappealing. She had lived with hunger so long she was no longer conscious of it. That afternoon she ate the pie and drank the milk so fast she was ashamed of herself. Marshall's mother would think they starved her at home. Her stomach ached later, but only because it had never been so full.

After that, the kitchen at Cedar Hill became her favorite place in all the world and Elizabeth Wayne her favorite person. Every anxiety faded away the moment she set foot on the linoleum floor and sat down at the oilcloth-covered table with her homework. Always there was something good to eat and the warm comfort of Elizabeth's presence nearby.

She had never known anyone as kind as Elizabeth, not even her grandmother, who in certain moods had a tongue like a lash and an eye as piercing as a stiletto. Such moods seemed inconceivable in Elizabeth. Her voice was gentle and her eyes too peaceful ever to possess such a look. They were the same soft brown as her hair, which she wore away from her face in a bun. Aly thought Elizabeth's hands were the loveliest she had ever seen. Their only adornment was a gold wedding band, narrow and plain but somehow very elegant on Elizabeth's slender finger.

Willy looked forward to Thursday afternoons, too. He and Sy Wayne were the best of friends. They played dominoes every week, and a delay with the ironing gave him the opportunity to go down to the barn for a visit. It also gave Aly the chance to feast her eyes on Marshall Wayne, if only for the few minutes it took him to wash his hands at the stainless steel sink or to drink a glass of water. He never said more than hello to her, and that at the prompting of his mother. "Say hello to Aly, son," Elizabeth would say, and Marshall, in a mumbled undertone, would grudgingly obey. He didn't like her, she knew, not because she was four years younger and skinny and plain but because she was a Kingston. That had been a fact she had just always known, like she knew that she was not loved as much as her older brother and sister.

The printing on the ticket cleared. The present returned. Marshall's eyes were still on her. Aly squirmed slightly under his direct scrutiny. Why didn't he look away? What about her had caught his attention? He couldn't possibly remember her. She herself could hardly remember the skinny, lank-haired little girl she had been back in the days of her mad crush on him. Then, with a little start, she realized he must find her attractive. Now *there* was an ironic twist that almost warranted making herself known.

Hello, Marshall. I'm Aly Kingston. Remember me? And what would she have said then if the deep brown eyes showed that he did not? *Don't you remember, Marshall? I'm the girl who lost Sampson for you. I'm the daughter of the man who foreclosed on your father's farm.* No, it wouldn't do. It wouldn't do at all. She would have to let him go, let the page stay missing from her life.

He had lit a cigarette, the smoke spiraling before his unwavering gaze. That, too, was new. Elizabeth would sigh in her grave if she knew. Her son, a smoker! Aly wondered if, for the sheer devilment of it, he intended to stare at her all through his call.

The announcement of her flight to Oklahoma City rescued her from a thirteenth reading of what to do should her luggage get lost, and she returned the ticket to her purse and gathered up her coat and overnight bag. Marshall turned back to the phone, and Aly stood up in relief, storing away a last picture of him before heading toward the departure gate.

A boarding line had already formed. She took her place at the end of it feeling a need to go back, knowing that she was letting something go that would never happen again. "May I see your ticket please?" the flight attendant asked, her eyes and smile on someone drawing up behind Aly. In confusion Aly realized she'd put the ticket back in her purse. Now she would have to juggle coat and luggage to get it.

"Allow me," said Marshall in a cool voice tinged with amusement, and took her case.

"Thank you," Aly murmured, going weak, rifling with undue fervor through her purse for the first-class ticket. Finally she located it and retrieved her case without meeting his eyes. Now a new sensation overcame her. *Marshall on the same plane*

bound for Oklahoma City? What did that mean? Did he have busi-
ness there? Or could he possibly be going on to Claiborne? Why?
Fear, sharp and cold, replaced the nebulous feelings of a while
ago.

"We're unusually crowded in first class today," the flight
attendant was saying to the three of them surrendering their
tickets and boarding passes. "Three A is the single here on the
aisle." She smiled at Aly. "And these"—her eyes moved past Aly
to Marshall and her smile warmed—"are the last two vacant
seats on the other side of the aisle in the rear. In the smoking
section."

"Thank you," said Aly quickly, sensing Marshall's disappointment as she slipped into the aisle seat. He and the woman
behind him, a voluble talker in a red coat, moved on past her to
the back section.

Once settled, Aly drew in toward the middle of the seats,
away from the aisle, and turned her gaze out the window. Her
abstraction was so complete that the flight attendant did not disturb her to take the coat folded on her lap. The plane began to
taxi down the runway. Presently it gathered speed and lifted off,
tearing through clouds almost immediately. Aly watched their
filmy drift for a while, then closed her eyes, feeling herself being
borne back into time. She was eighteen again. It was the first of
June, and she was driving her graduation present, a smart little
sports car, out to Cedar Hill…

Chapter Two

As Aly parked in front of the old clapboard farmhouse, she looked briefly toward the space between two large pecan trees, a habit begun when the ancient pickup Marshall had driven in high school signaled that he was home. Today her automatic glance extended into a long stare of surprise. The black second-hand Ford that had replaced the pickup when he went off to college was parked between the trees.

Marshall was home! But why? Finals at Wharton, Elizabeth had told her, were next week. And then, at last, he would graduate from the finest business school in the country. Perplexed, Aly remained behind the wheel of her new car and considered what could possibly have dragged Marshall away from his books at such a crucial time. She knew of no one who was sick or who had died. Could good news have brought him home to Claiborne? She hadn't heard of any, but she certainly didn't want to contribute a negative note by lugging in a basket of wash for Elizabeth's ironing board. Not when she knew how Marshall felt about his mother having to do such work to make ends meet, especially for the Kingstons.

Besides, she looked the mess she usually did. If she'd only known he would be home, she would have tried to do something to her hair, her face—worn something other than cutoff jeans and a T-shirt. Not that Marshall would have noticed. He never had. He had a special look for the Kingstons, a way of looking right through them, clear out to the other side, as if they didn't exist. It was a type of disdain particularly nettlesome to Victoria, Aly's older sister and Marshall's classmate. "Somebody ought to take him down a notch or two." Nobody ever did.

But, Aly sighed, if she didn't pick up the ironing today, her father would be deprived of his weekly supply of perfect shirts. She'd be sure to get that long look of silent reproof that she couldn't stand. Maybe today Elizabeth had the ironing ready to pick up, and she could depart without any to-do. She'd leave the basket of wash in the car and bring it back tomorrow when Marshall was gone. Surely he wouldn't be staying long, not with finals next week.

Through the door's oval pane of age-discolored glass, Aly saw Elizabeth coming up the breezeway that ran through the center of the house. Aly's misgivings increased when she noted Elizabeth's slow walk and bowed head, as if the weight of the thick, graying twist of hair on her neck were too much for her. Fear fluttered in Aly's stomach. Ordinarily, despite the clumsy, brown oxfords she wore summer and winter, Elizabeth's step would have been light, her saintly face alight with welcome for her Thursday visitor. Something must have happened to Marshall.

"Elizabeth, what's the matter?" Aly asked at once when the door opened and she saw the tired, red-rimmed eyes of her friend.

"Aly—" Elizabeth spoke painfully. "I-it's bad news."

"What kind of bad news?"

"Tell her, Mother." The voice, tense and deep, came from Marshall, who suddenly appeared beside his mother and glared down at Aly. Aly lifted an awestruck face. Tall and athletically slim, with eyes as richly dark as her mother's sable coat, Marshall Wayne had always been the most handsome boy she'd ever seen. But between the glimpse she'd had of him last Christmas and now, maturity had added a new dimension, a force and power that almost overwhelmed.

"You do not look at Marshall Wayne," one of her friends once declared, "you *behold* him." Beholding him now, noticing the hard new manliness of his features and form, she felt an odd sense of loss. He had gone, the boy who had grown up in this house. She would never again see the Marshall Wayne she had loved since the first grade.

She tore away her gaze to ask of Elizabeth, "Tell me what?"

But Marshall answered with a flash of clenched teeth, "Your father intends to foreclose on us. We got a notice from the courthouse. We have thirty days to come up with the money we owe the bank or the farm will be posted for auction."

Stunned, Aly stared at Elizabeth for confirmation. "But that's impossible! My dad wouldn't foreclose on Cedar Hill."

"I'm afraid you're wrong, Aly," Elizabeth answered in weary resignation. "We haven't been able to keep up with even the interest on the principal for some time. We're way behind in our payments. Marshall came home to try to get his father to declare bankruptcy rather than to let the bank foreclose, but Sy won't hear of it."

Aly still could not believe it. "There's been a mistake," she declared obstinately. "What would the bank want with Cedar Hill?"

Moving his mother gently aside, Marshall stepped through the door. "That's what I intend to find out," he said furiously. Aly backed away, awed as much by his new grandeur as by his rage.

"Where are you going, son?" Elizabeth asked anxiously.

"To see Lorne Kingston," he replied, making for the porch steps. "He's going to explain why he wants our farm!"

Aly, after a moment's hesitation, propelled her thin, sun-browned legs after him. "Marshall—" she called, following him down the steps and across the yard. "Let me go with you. Maybe I can talk to him."

Without altering his pace, Marshall laughed bitterly. "You think your father would listen to you, Aly? You?"

She winced from his taunt, but she persisted. "You won't get in to see him without me," she warned. "Dad will be expecting you. He's probably already alerted the security guards. I may not be able to talk him into changing his mind, but I can at least get you into his office."

Marshall halted to consider her argument, holding her gaze thoughtfully. Then suddenly, as if he'd never really seen it before, the brown eyes shifted in curious study of her face. Embarrassment seared through her. She had read the same expression on the faces of so many. *No, she didn't look at all like a Kingston*, she was always tempted to say. She was well aware of the joke that explained her presence in the Kingston household—that at birth she had been placed in the wrong crib at the hospital. She showed how little she cared by working hard at being as unlike any other member of her family as possible.

But now, having caught Marshall's attention for the first time in her eighteen years, she wished she'd agreed to braces for her slightly protruding teeth, to a permanent for her hair, to the cream that Victoria vowed would vanish the pox of freckles covering her face. She wished she could have forced down Annie Jo's unappetizing fare at home, the monotonous lunches at school. Then there might have been some curves to her figure, something to improve the lines of her T-shirt and jeans.

"Why don't you ever curl your hair?" Marshall asked suddenly, impatiently flicking aside her bangs, touching her for the first time in their lives. "How do you see with that mop hanging down in your eyes?"

The bangs had been her one attempt to conceal her freckles, especially abundant on her forehead. "I—I'm going to the barbershop next week."

The dark brows quirked in reluctant humor. "The barbershop?"

"It gets Mother's goat for me to go to a barber."

"God, Aly, why do you cut off your nose to spite your face? All right," he said, his tone taking them back to business, "come on then. You drive your car, and I'll take mine."

Aly followed the Ford in her sports car, her eyes never straying from the dark head in front of her. Blast her father! If this were true, the Kingstons would never be able to dig out of this hole with Marshall. She could read his hate and anger for anything remotely connected with the family name in every rigid movement of the broad shoulders, every turn of the sculpted profile. For the moment at least, she would not allow herself even to consider a foreclosure on Cedar Hill—what it would mean to the Waynes and to herself. She still believed there had been a mistake. What could her father possibly want with a farm? Farmland wasn't selling right now, and Cedar Hill was too far out of Claiborne to be developed as commercial property. It wasn't as if the bank couldn't afford to let the Waynes ride for a while. The oil boom had the Kingston State Bank flourishing. Other farmers were allowed an extensive grace period during bad financial times. Why not Sy Wayne? This whole thing had to be a mistake. Surely her father wasn't intending to foreclose on Cedar Hill.

But Aly knew too well the president and chairman of the Kingston State Bank, and depression hung over her like a dark cloud by the time they drove into the bank's parking lot. Marshall helped himself to one of the two spots marked president and chairman, the shabby black Ford a seedy contrast to her father's new white Lincoln Continental in the other. Aly had to hurry to catch up with Marshall's fast stride, reaching him as he threw open both of the heavy glass doors at once and strode defiantly toward her father's office in the rear of the bank. Their entrance attracted the immediate and fascinated attention of the tellers and employees at desks around the room. Aly could tell from their expressions that news of the foreclosure was out. By tonight it would be discussed at every supper table in town.

Mrs. Devers, her father's secretary of many years, observed Marshall with stern disapproval. She could not see Aly, only a pair of extremely thin legs in tattered jean shorts behind him. "Yes, young man, what is it?"

"I want to see the senior Lorne Kingston."

"Do you have an appointment?"

"He doesn't need one, Mrs. Devers," said Aly, stepping from behind Marshall. "We're together."

"So I see," pursed Mrs. Devers critically. "Your father is busy at the moment, Aly. He doesn't wish to be disturbed."

"Too bad," said Aly, sailing past the older woman's desk. "Come on, Marshall."

Lorne Kingston Sr.—warned by two sharp buzzes of the intercom that trouble was on the way—was already rising from behind his desk when Aly and Marshall entered. Buttoning his coat over a flawlessly ironed shirt, he said, "I can't say that I'm surprised to see you, Marshall, even though I understood from your father that you were busy studying for your finals."

"Is that why you waited until this week to have the sheriff serve notice of an intent to foreclose?"

Lorne Kingston—tall, graying, imperious—straightened

slim shoulders. "You flatter yourself. I fear you've wasted valuable time on a useless trip if you've come home to convince me to change my mind about foreclosing. I'm sure, however, that your coming has been a comfort to your folks." His glance cut sharply to Aly, taking in the T-shirt and ragged-edged jeans. "Young lady, the family asks so little of you. Is it too much to expect you not to come into this bank unless you are suitably attired?"

Stunned that the bank did indeed plan to foreclose, Aly replied in amazement, "This is an emergency."

"Your appearance will do little to aid it. Now, Marshall, have your say and get out. I'm a busy man."

Marshall's dark eyes flashed. "I want to know why you want Cedar Hill."

"Frankly, I don't want it. The place will be a liability to the bank until it's sold. All we want out of it is our vested interest in it. As I explained to Sy, anything over and above will be returned to him as equity. That's a promise."

"Even if the bank buys it at auction and sells it later for a profit?"

"Yes. I think even you would agree that's more than fair. And until we do find a buyer, your family is welcome to stay on the land and pay us minimal rent. Naturally, the stock, equipment, and crops will be sold at auction. Now is there anything else?"

Her father's generosity astonished Aly. Ordinarily in a foreclosure, the bank pocketed all profits above the note value. The excess was never returned to the mortgagee, not by the Kingston State Bank. Knowing her father, she figured the offer must have been made to preserve the bank's image in Claiborne. Residents would not look kindly upon the foreclosure of Cedar Hill. Her throat tightened as she looked at Marshall. He seemed to be having trouble with his next words.

"Yes—I—it's about Sampson," he said a little less steadily. "Matt Taylor has offered me six thousand for him. I've accepted a position at the Chase Manhattan Bank after graduation. If you'll take the money from Matt to pay the interest in arrears, I'll use every cent I can spare from my salary to pay off the debt...."

"Sampson?" Aly interrupted in disbelief. "You would sell Sampson? But—but, Marshall, you can't. You love that horse!"

"Stay out of this, Aly!" he snapped, his eyes still on Lorne. "How about it, Mr. Kingston."

"No." The word fired out bullet-quick.

"No?" Aly echoed in surprise. "But why not, Dad? Marshall isn't asking for anything but a chance to pay back the bank."

"I said no. The bank has given Sy that chance for years. And to grant an extension based on a promise that you would meet the farm's obligations, Marshall, is ridiculous. The board would laugh me out of my president's chair. You're a young man. You'll find that every cent you earn will be needed to meet your own expenses in these first years of working, especially in New York. You'll need clothes, a place to live. You'll have transportation and social expenses, insurances—an endless list to devour your salary."

"Mr. Kingston." Marshall stepped closer, his tone modified, and Aly held her breath at the plea she heard in it. "You control the board. This bank is yours. Whatever you say goes. If you suggest an extension, the directors will go along with it. That farm represents my parents' lives. My dad will never be able to hold his head up again if he loses it. Also—" Here Marshall had to run a tongue over dry lips. "He's got a bad heart, Mr. Kingston. Moving away from Cedar Hill, taking my mother away from the house she loves, could literally kill him. I'll do anything—sacrifice anything to pay off their debt if you'll just

15

give us a little more time." Aly, wide-eyed with the certain knowledge of what was coming next, shrank inside herself when she heard him force out, "Please don't foreclose, Mr. Kingston. I'm begging you."

She caught the glittering triumph that appeared briefly in her father's gray eyes and despised him utterly in that moment.

"No, Marshall." Lorne shook his head implacably. "I'm afraid you must take some of the blame for this. I warned Sy when he remortgaged the farm to send you to Wharton that the bank would not be lenient again if he fell behind in his payments. You could have gone to any number of less expensive schools on the scholarships you were offered. But no, Sy had to have the best for his son. Well, I hope the price was worth it. Now you must excuse me. I have work to do...."

"Damn you." Marshall grated, color mounting beneath the smooth olive skin of his face. He stepped threateningly closer to Lorne and jabbed a finger into the silk tie. "You know that remortgage was your idea. You knew he wouldn't be able to meet his note. You promised him that the bank would carry him if he fell behind in his payments. You intended all along to foreclose. Now I want to know why. Why do you want Cedar Hill?"

"Get away from me, you impertinent ingrate," ordered Lorne angrily, his thin nostrils flaring, "or I will have you arrested for assault, and you can spend exam week in jail. That should do wonders for that illustrious grade point average, which now seems to have been earned at too great a sacrifice. Just how did you think your father got the money to send you to Wharton, I'd like to know?"

Not moving, Marshall said, "He told me he had some old World War II bonds stashed away."

"A regrettable deception, apparently," said Lorne dryly, obviously relieved at the entrance of two security guards, men who had been Marshall's football teammates in high school. "Your father could have declared bankruptcy," the banker reminded him. "Then he would have retained everything."

"You knew damn well Dad's pride wouldn't let him do that. You banked on it—literally."

"Ah, well, that's to your sorrow. Pride is a luxury your family has never learned it cannot afford, Marshall. Now your friends here will see you to the door." He nodded to the two young men, who began a reluctant approach to Marshall. "Alyson," Lorne said to her sharply, "you will remain."

"Do you think I'm dressed for it?" she asked coldly, earning an irate glance from her father.

"Tom...Clay...You can cool it. I'm going," Marshall said without taking his eyes off Lorne. "But first I have something to say to our town's leading citizen here. You're going to pay for this, Kingston," he vowed through clenched teeth. "It may take years to get you, but you can be assured I will. You're going to regret the day your greed ever led you to foreclose on Cedar Hill. That's a promise you can count on."

Lorne drew back slightly but returned the hostile look. "That sounds very much like a threat, Marshall, and made in the presence of witnesses, too. You'd better hope I'm never the victim of foul play. You'd be the first one suspected."

"I doubt that. I have the feeling I'd be standing somewhere back in a long line."

Aly saw her father's lips whiten. "Get out," he said with glacial restraint. "Get out now, Marshall. Aly, don't you dare leave."

Oblivious to the lecture her father was delivering to her back, Aly stood at the window overlooking the parking lot and watched Marshall talking with his two friends. She maintained an obstinate silence, hoping her father's wrath would play out before Marshall left. Her sympathy would mean nothing, she knew, but she just had to tell him that all was not lost. Already she was conceiving a plan that might soften this blow.

Released at last, she hurried outside to find the security guards gone and Marshall fixedly contemplating the white Continental. With a face like sculpted stone, he vowed softly before she could speak, "Someday, Aly, my car—my Lincoln—will be in that spot. Someday I will be the president and chairman of this bank."

His words carried total, blood-chilling conviction. Aly stared at him, forgetting what she had planned to say. Then, abruptly, without glancing at her, he went around to the driver's side of his car and got in.

"Marshall—" Holding back her bangs with one hand, she bent down to the window while he started the motor. "I—I'm so ashamed, so sorry..."

He looked up at her, the brown eyes opaque with desolation. "I know you are, Aly. This has nothing to do with you. You shouldn't feel in the least responsible."

Aly drew up, feeling a little better. She stepped back and watched him drive away, knowing what an effort it cost him to take the turn out of the parking lot at a judicious speed. But then Marshall Wayne was noted for his cool head. He'd never let anger make a fool out of him. She glanced toward the Lincoln Continental. There was not a doubt in her mind that he meant what he said.

That evening Aly confronted her father in the study. "Now that you've said your piece, I intend to say mine," she declared. "You've been guilty of some pretty underhanded tricks, Dad, but this one takes the cake."

"You watch your tongue, young lady, or—"

"Or what? You'll take away my car? I'll walk. But if I walk, I talk. And boy, would I have plenty to say."

"Aly, as I explained to Marshall, the Waynes have been carried on the bank's debit rolls for years. What else could I do? I knew Marshall ought to go to Wharton. But Wharton is expensive. I told Sy that. I pleaded with him to send his boy to Oklahoma University."

"O.U.? For a student like Marshall? You've got to be kidding, Dad. Marshall Wayne has the most exceptional mind that ever graduated from Claiborne High School. He's Ivy League material through and through. Why didn't you just set him up a college fund at the bank? Then he could have paid it off when he got out of school. That would have been the truly charitable thing to do."

When her father offered no comment on her suggestion, Aly continued. "But you wanted the Wayne land, didn't you? And Marshall's education was a way to get it. You approached Sy with the idea first, talked him into sending Marshall to Wharton. How would Sy, just a poor Oklahoma farmer, have known of such a place? To help his brilliant son off to a good start in life, you suggested he remortgage the farm. That way Sy wouldn't think he was accepting charity. Then, when he wasn't able to meet his note, you would step in and foreclose, something that Sy never anticipated because you promised otherwise. Who's going to buy that land from you, Dad? Some development company coming into Claiborne with its first mall?"

Lorne Kingston flicked an imaginary ash from the red brocade smoking jacket he affected for after-dinner wear. Rolling an expensive cigar lovingly between his lips, he regarded his daughter. He had never been able to understand it. The only one of his children whose company he actually enjoyed was his youngest, plainest, and most aggravating child. Aly was in many ways exactly like him—bold, perceptive, and intelligent—descriptions that would not apply to his other two, more physically appealing children. But Aly possessed other characteristics he could not claim: compassion, integrity, and loyalty. They made for a certain obstinance in his daughter that had always set them at odds with one another but never quite estranged them.

Yet, oddly enough, only in her presence could he completely relax, be himself, without pretense, for he had nothing to lose or gain with Aly. She would never love him more; she would never love him less. Only with her could he enjoy a feeling of total honesty. Waving the cigar, he indicated she take the companion chair to his.

"Too far out of town for a mall," he said as she sat down. "You will know my plans when it is time. I would have thought you would be praising my generosity in allowing the Waynes to stay on the farm until a buyer can be found." He puffed the cigar serenely.

"Your generosity always pays you higher dividends than the recipient, Dad. You know the Waynes won't stay on land belonging to somebody else. They'll be off as soon as possible, though where they'll go, what they'll do, I don't know. I had no idea Sy suffered from heart trouble."

"Oh, Marshall just tossed that in as a sympathy plea. Sy Wayne is as healthy as a horse. Marshall is learning the banker's trick of bending the truth a bit in order to get his way. He should know better than to try it with me."

"Sy and Elizabeth's son would never bend the truth to get his way. You shouldn't measure everybody by yourself, Dad. One thing for sure, Marshall will just die if his father has to go to work for somebody else."

"I doubt that. Your young Marshall is a tough customer. I

predict he will do very well in the business world, go far. The farther away from here, the better."

"I'm glad you recognize that, Dad. Marshall may just be in the position someday to carry out that promise he made you."

Lorne smiled. "Once he has a taste of money and luxury, of big-city living, he'll be too busy enjoying the good life and paying its bills to come back to a little Oklahoma town to even any scores. Money and success have a way of corrupting even the most determined motives."

"Not vengeance," declared Aly. "Not if it's personal enough, and you can believe that foreclosing on Cedar Hill is personal enough."

Apprehension, light and minnow-quick, darted through Lorne's self-satisfaction. It was gone in a flash. "Anything else you wanted to see me about?" he asked abruptly.

"Yes. I want to borrow against my inheritance," Aly stated, referring to the sizable bequest left her by her grandmother, the woman who had given birth to this bank vault that was Aly's father.

The cigar bobbed in surprise. "What for?"

"I want to buy Cedar Hill."

The cigar dropped from Lorne's mouth. Hastily, he retrieved it before the luxurious brocade could be damaged, then scowled at his daughter. "No!" he answered. "Absolutely, unequivocally no!"

"Then I want to borrow against it to buy Sampson. The money will help the Waynes relocate, maybe provide a down payment on another place until Marshall can help out."

"You don't know the first thing about horses."

"I can learn. Willy can teach me."

"Willy has refused to go near a horse for twenty years. Furthermore, you have no place to stable Sampson."

"I'll find a place. If you don't let me borrow against my inheritance, then when I come into my trust, I'll draw out all my money and deposit it in your competitor's bank. Think how that would affect your image as a banker and a father, not to mention the bank's assets."

Lorne puffed rapidly and almost laughed, realizing she had him boxed in. He hadn't any doubt that if he refused her the money, Aly at twenty-four would do exactly as threatened. He had never forgiven his mother for leaving the lion's share of her fortune to Aly. It had been the one major financial reversal in his long business life. "All right," he agreed, "but you needn't think I'll extend you credit or increase your allowance for feeding and stabling expenses. You better figure out a way to afford a horse. And I'd give a little thought to the possibility that Marshall might not sell to you, you being a Kingston and all." He smiled complacently.

Aly stood up to go. "I'll let you know the amount I want to borrow—"

"Six thousand, five hundred. Not a cent over."

"Now, Dad, you know that wouldn't go far toward the purchase of another place for the Waynes. Besides, Sampson is worth a lot more than that. Matt Taylor was practically stealing him."

As she neared the door, her father startled her by saying, "Do you suppose you will ever outgrow your obsession for Marshall Wayne? He could never be interested in anyone like you, you know. And once Cedar Hill is sold, the Waynes will probably have to leave Claiborne. There's no work around here for a man like Sy, no place to live. They'll probably want to leave anyway. That damnable Wayne pride won't let Sy keep his family in a town where they're at the mercy of local pity and charity. Chances are, after the auction, you may never see Marshall again."

How was it possible that after all these years, her father could still hurt her? She thought herself inured to him. But she wasn't, she found. "That possibility pleases you, doesn't it, Dad. Did you by any chance foreclose on Cedar Hill to hurt me?"

"My dear," said Lorne, his tone softly chiding, "I never once thought of you in regard to the foreclosure on Cedar Hill."

Chapter Three

The bustle of the flight attendants as they began serving drinks to the first-class passengers failed to penetrate Aly's reverie. Not until the smartly aproned young woman tapped her shoulder, and her seat mate snapped his tray table down, did the question she'd just been asked register, bringing Aly back to the present with a jolt.

"What?"

The hostess patiently repeated her litany. "May I serve you a cocktail, some wine, or a soft drink?"

"Oh, no, thank you. Nothing for me." Aly rested her head against the seat back again as the attendant supplied a Bloody Mary and a miniature tray of cheese and crackers to the man in the window seat.

Marshall, from his vantage point three rows back and across the aisle, watched the elegant young woman sigh and close her eyes again.

As soon as they were airborne, Marshall had drawn a polite but definite curtain between himself and his garrulous seat mate, then adjusted the back of his seat to get a better view of the woman he had first noticed in the airport. There was something naggingly familiar about her. At first he had been charmed by her embarrassment that he had caught her staring at him. He was unused to that kind of reaction from women of her age and…liberated modernity, he supposed he'd call it. Most would have continued to stare boldly, invitingly, issuing a kind of challenge that lately he had come to find less and less provocative. He had been a little touched by her disconcertion and had treated himself to an inspection of his own while she pretended such interest in her ticket, noticing then how really lovely she was. Her figure had the certain long-lined elegance that he always associated with the sleek grace of a thoroughbred, an impression he thought was further heightened by her clothes, an elegant tweed suit with a simple white blouse. And the way she wore her hair, a full, sun-streaked mane of it, golden and glorious. Now he felt sure he knew her. Could she be from Claiborne? Then why hadn't she recognized him? He hadn't changed that much in thirteen years. Of course, this woman—he guessed her age to be about thirty—would have been eighteen or so when he left Claiborne, not likely to remember him since he would have been away at Wharton while she was in high school. And he couldn't recall any eighteen-year-old who had shown the promise of this woman's kind of beauty. Still…something about the small nose, the firm little chin made him think he knew her. She was unmarried, he noticed from her ringless left hand resting on the armrest. It was a pleasing, capable hand with buffed, well-trimmed nails, the kind of hand that diamonds would not suit.

His mother's had been like that. He still had the simple gold wedding band she had asked him to keep shortly before she died. "A special girl waits for you, son, the kind of girl who will want this ring around her finger." He had never met that special girl, and none of the women he knew would want a plain, gold band. Its simple eloquence would be lost on them. Somehow he knew that it would not be lost on the woman up the aisle.

He closed his eyes. He could simply inquire, of course, but her manner had made it plain that she would not encourage conversation from a stranger on a plane, even one she clearly found disturbing. He would just wait and see if she got off in Oklahoma City. Someone from home he recognized might be meeting her plane.

Home. A misnomer when applied to Claiborne. He couldn't call Claiborne home. His parents were dead, his birthplace demolished, Cedar Hill laid to waste, most of his friends moved away—all the ties that bind cut long ago. Even so, more and more often he found his thoughts back in Oklahoma, buried in the past. It had begun—this going back—one cold January day in New York over a year ago. His accountant had handed him his balance sheet, smiled, and asked, "How does it feel to know you don't have to work another day in your life to be able to enjoy it to the fullest?"

He had studied the polished toe of a hand-sewn shoe, one of many pairs that occupied a closet filled with equally expensive custom suits, and considered an answer. "Cheated," he had replied at last to the astonished man, "very cheated."

On the way back to his bachelor apartment on the Upper East Side, he had thought on his reply and decided, feeling slightly disillusioned, that the view from the top was never as good as expected on the climb up. He had found it so with everything he had attained: money, position, possessions, women. Always there was disappointment. The glow did not last, and afterward the darkness was deeper than before.

But this strange disappointment had come to exist only at the periphery of the main objective in his life, a goal he had been pursuing singe-mindedly since his graduation from Wharton. This disappointment did not affect his pursuit in the least. The accomplishment of this goal would be different—would not disappoint, only elate and fulfill him, and he could hardly wait. Marshall smiled to himself. He hoped they thought he'd forgotten—the Kingstons. Their surprise would make his victory all the sweeter.

In the front of the plane, Aly glanced at her seat mate happily munching away on packaged cheese spread and seed-speckled crackers. Though the days of positive distaste for nourishment were behind her, the sight of the airline-furnished treat caused a familiar feeling of revulsion she hadn't experienced in years. So much was coming back that she hadn't felt in years. She wondered what Marshall was thinking, this close to Claiborne, if the past and its feelings were as fresh and poignant to him as they were to her. Was he, too, remembering that awful time he had come home to confront her father? She closed her eyes again, slipping from the first-class cabin back to her bedroom and the morning after the scene at the bank.

She was dreaming. In the dream she was still in grade school, and her mother had a ton of laundry for Willy to deliver this afternoon, just like last week; and maybe Elizabeth hadn't gotten to it all, and they would have to wait for the last few pieces to be ironed. She hoped so. She would be able to finish her biology notebook on the kitchen table and wait for *him* to come in the back door from his chores.

And, as if seeing Marshall weren't enough, this was the Thursday of the month his mother always baked apple pies, one for supper and one for the freezer. Nobody in the world baked apple pies better than Marshall's mother, and Aly would be given a big, juicy slice to enjoy while Elizabeth finished the last of her dad's long-sleeved white shirts...

"Aly, wake up! Get up, you hear me! Willy has quit!"

Aly woke with a start, her heart thudding sickeningly from having been jerked from the peace of her favorite dream.

"Annie Jo, for heaven's sake!" she complained. "Don't you know a person can have a heart attack being yanked awake like that?"

"Willy's quit. He must have just up and left early this morning!"

"What?" Aly threw off the covers and sprang out of bed. "What are you talking about?"

Annie Jo, a thin black woman whose placid countenance and smooth skin belied her hard forty years, wrung her slender hands and repeated piteously, "Willy's quit. I just found out. Somethin' about your pa's foreclosure on the Waynes. His room's been cleaned out, and he left a note sayin' he wouldn't be back."

Aly slipped into a robe and regarded her family's cook and maid with compassion. Annie Jo and Willy had fought like cats and dogs for twenty years, mainly because of Annie Jo's cooking, but they were genuinely fond and protective of each other. "I'm not surprised, Annie Jo. Fact is, I don't know why Dad didn't anticipate Willy leaving. He and Sy Wayne are the best of friends, and Willy wouldn't be one to stomach what Dad has done. Did the note say where he had gone?"

"Only that Mr. Kingston could send what he owed him to the Waynes. Oh, Aly, this place ain't goin' to be the same without Willy. It'll be lonesome enough when you go off to college," she wailed.

Aly put her arms around the woman. "I'm not going anywhere, Annie Jo, so don't worry about that. I'll get dressed and go out to Cedar Hill. Maybe I can talk Willy into coming back."

But she rather doubted it, Aly thought moments later as she

came down the stairs. In the dining room her family was assembling for the ritual of breakfast, presided over by Eleanor Kingston, Aly's mother. "Good morning, all," Aly said, entering and heading for the silver coffeepot on the sideboard. Nothing was yet on the table. She wondered if Annie Jo had charred the bacon, burned the toast, and overcooked the eggs before or after she had been told about Willy. Probably before, Aly judged, as Annie Jo came through the swinging door with breakfast platters showing congealed grease.

"Willy has left us, Aly," said her brother, Lorne Junior. "The nerve of that guy. After all we've done for him."

"Nobody believes in gratitude or loyalty anymore," complained Eleanor at her head of the table. At fifty, she was still a beautiful and stylish woman with a head-turning figure. Her delicate features and blond hair, long-lashed blue eyes and full breasts had been inherited by her first daughter, Victoria, who was away finishing her last semester of college.

Aly sipped her coffee. "It was precisely gratitude and loyalty that caused Willy to leave. Sy Wayne is his friend. He could never work for someone who had pulled the rug out from under his buddy."

"As usual, you're allowing sentiment to cloud the facts, Aly," Lorne Junior remonstrated. "Dad didn't pull the rug out from under Sy Wayne. Foreclosure happens when money lent in good faith is not repaid."

"If you say so, Lorne Junior," said Aly, glancing at her father, who was reading the paper with an air of unconcern. She rather liked her brother, an amiable soul whose only drawbacks were his slow intellect and blind devotion to their father. Eight years older than she, Lorne Junior had managed, just barely, to graduate from college with a degree in banking. Being groomed to take over his father's position as president and chairman when he retired, he lived at home, content with his room on the top floor of the family's impressive three-story house, his private entrance, and the lack of responsibility for his own meals, laundry, and housekeeping. He drove a Porsche, which he had ordered in a conservative gray, and planned to marry in due time the daughter of a local insurance man. The pathway before him he saw as wide, straight, and unimpeded. If he had a worry, it was simply that he lacked the perspicacity of his father in banking matters, but experience and time would make up for that. In thirteen years when his father planned to retire, he would be ready to step into his shoes.

"It's not every family," he reminded his sister, "who would hire a cripple."

"Certainly not for what we paid Willy," Aly agreed. "The law would come after them."

"Aly, sit down and eat your breakfast," Eleanor ordered, pressing delicate, rose-tipped fingers to her temples. "I have a headache from all this."

"Sorry, Mother," Aly apologized lightly, taking a seat near her father, who, she knew, had missed not a word.

Drinking her orange juice and swallowing the vitamins that probably prevented what would later come to be known as anorexia, she nibbled indifferently at a piece of cold toast. Because she seemed healthy enough at her yearly physicals, her mother never badgered her to gain weight, blaming Aly's extreme thinness on a chemical disposition inherited from her husband's side of the family. "Food doesn't take with you, Aly, because you have the Kingston metabolism. Like your father, you will always be thin." Such had not been the lot of the other children, who took after Eleanor in their tendency to gain weight. Eleanor never seemed to notice that Aly simply could not force down Annie Jo's meals and complaints about the cafeteria food fell on deaf ears. Mass-produced snack and fast foods held no appeal either, so Aly subsisted on vitamins, juice, fruit, and milk. Her father and brother, she knew, managed their nutritional requirements by dining daily on the home-cooked lunch specials at Willard's Cafe down from the bank.

"Have you thought any more about where you will keep Sampson when you buy him?" Lorne asked, folding the paper and laying it aside to salt and pepper his eggs.

"At one of the stables around town."

"None of them have their own paddock. You'd have to go out every day to exercise the horse, and you don't even know how to ride."

"I can learn."

"Alyson, I think it is much too dangerous for you to own that horse," Eleanor interjected, her ivory brow peevishly creased from the grievances of the morning. "This is just a whim of yours that will cause no end of inconvenience. Once the novelty of owning that horse wears off, you'll wind up selling him anyway. Who will look after him when you go to college?"

"Mother, how many times must I tell you? I'm not going to college."

Lorne, seeing his wife's feathers about to ruffle, took the subject back to Sampson. "Have you any idea what kind of time is involved in caring for a horse? You'll have to check on him daily, make sure he's being fed and watered properly. You'll have to exercise and groom him. I'm just stating the concerns that will be bothering Marshall. Even if you weren't a Kingston, he might not want to sell Sampson to you. He will probably prefer to see the horse left with someone like Matt Taylor, who has a financial interest in taking care of him, even if Marshall has to sell him for less than the generous offer I'm sure you'll make him."

"How much of a generous offer?" Lorne Junior wanted to know.

Aly, ignoring the question, got up and threw down her napkin in a childish gesture, which she realized would not help her cause. But it was all just so overwhelming—Willy leaving, her family's attitude, and the foreclosure of the most wonderful place on earth. "I'm buying Sampson," she declared, her bottom lip trembling. "Nobody could take better care of him than I will. I'll find a place to stable him, just don't you worry."

"Well," said her father serenely, "I believe I'll just wait to hear that Marshall will sell you Sampson before I draw up any papers. And when you get out to the Waynes' this morning," he added as she headed for the door, "tell Willy that he can expect no reference from me to find another job."

Aly stopped short and turned back to stare at her father. She opened her mouth to say something, then clamped it shut. What was the use? Fairness was asking too much of a Kingston.

On the way out to the farm, vestiges of the dream from which she'd been awakened still clung, provoking poignant memories not so long past. Aly recalled the first time she had ever seen Cedar Hill. She had been six years old, sitting in the backseat of the family Cadillac with Willy at the wheel. In a town of fifteen thousand, Aly and Victoria had the distinction of being the only children driven to and from school by a chauffeur, a fact made indisputably clear by the black-billed hat Eleanor insisted Willy wear on such occasions.

One Thursday when Victoria had chosen to ride home with Lorne Junior, then a sophomore with his first car, Willy turned left out of the school parking lot rather than right.

"Where we going, Willy?"

"Out to Cedar Hill. Your mother wants me to deliver the

wash and pick up the ironing every Thursday after school from now on because of the gas shortage."

"The farm where Marshall Wayne lives?"

"Uh-huh. You know him?"

"Just by sight. He's a fifth grader."

But she knew who he was, all right. Everybody did, and all her friends and even her sister, who was also in the fifth grade, had a crush on him. At ten years old, Marshall was the best-looking boy in elementary school and the quarterback of the pee wee football team. That he kept to himself and rarely smiled—Victoria called him stuck up—didn't seem to detract from his popularity. Aly kept waiting for him to notice her beautiful sister, but he never did. As she and Willy drove out to the Wayne farm that day, she wondered how long it would take Victoria to snag him.

It had been the first of May, and the corn was high and beginning to tassel, a month away from picking time. It grew right up to the cyclone fence that ran around the Waynes' front yard, an area of sparse grass long discouraged by the shade of two giant pecan trees.

While Willy went inside with the laundry basket, she had stayed in the car and inspected with interest the place where Marshall lived. She decided the name of the farm came from cedars planted as windbreakers along the periphery of the knoll where the house stood. The farmhouse, a clapboard frame, was old, she knew. Her history book had described the style as coming to rural America in the early 1900s. She had visited similar houses and knew that the porch that skirted three sides was screened in the back for a summer parlor. This one featured the usual porch swing as well as a hospitable-looking table placed between two flat-armed porch chairs and pots of pretty red geraniums lining the broad steps. Twin chimneys faced each other from the left and right ends of the house; and in the center, a long, wide hall divided the bedrooms and bath on one side from the front parlor, dining room, and kitchen on the other. It was called a breezeway and served as exactly that in the summer months when the front door with its long oval pane of glass remained open so the air could circulate freely through the center of the structure. The house could have used a new roof and a fresh coat of yellow paint, but unlike most of its kind, whose porches sagged with clutter, and chickens scratched among rusting cans and farm equipment in the yard, the Wayne property had a tidy, well-cared-for look—like Marshall's patched jeans and worn shoes.

"Poor dirt farmers," the Waynes were called by people like her family, and Aly sensed that Marshall minded. She perceived very early that it was pride, not conceit, that kept him aloof, his head held high and dark eyes brooding.

That afternoon while Willy was still inside, the bus from the elementary school drove up at the end of the lane and deposited Marshall. Aly responded to her friends, who had spotted the Cadillac and were hollering and waving from the windows as if they hadn't seen her for a week. She would have spoken to Marshall, if he'd given her so much as a glance. But he had walked past the car without turning his head and gone into the house as if she and the Cadillac were invisible.

"Why don't you offer a ride to young Marshall next Thursday, since we're coming out to his place anyway?" Willy suggested on their way home. "He'd probably prefer the Caddy to the bus."

"Somehow I don't think you're right about that, Willy, but I'll ask."

The next day on the playground, Marshall looked through her as if she'd been a screen door and said, "No thanks."

"Willy," she asked not long afterward, "why don't the Waynes cotton to us Kingstons?"

"Well, now, Punkin, there's an old saying that borrowing is not much better than beggin', and the Waynes have been borrowing from your dad for a long time. Just as they're about to get a nickel ahead, somethin' comes along—like drought or inflation or a gas shortage—that costs a dime. It bothers Sy awfully that he's not his own man and that his wife has to take in ironing, not that Elizabeth seems to mind."

"It bothers Marshall, too."

"Oh, does it ever. He takes poverty personally, that one does, and he's straining at the bit to do something about it. Give him time and he will, too."

That summer she continued to accompany Willy on "laundry day," happy to sit in the back of the Cadillac with the windows rolled down, absorbing the sights and smells and sounds of the country, feeling the constant tightness between her shoulder blades melt away. Sometimes they didn't get out to the farm until twilight, a time when she would generally be rewarded with the sight of Marshall—or at least the top of his dark head—leading the cows through the green corn to the barn to be milked.

Her senses were never more stimulated than at dusk on Cedar Hill in summer. By then the crickets were in full voice and the fireflies were out. From the house, the aroma of supper cooking drifted out to mingle with the soft evening smells of dew and earth and growing things. Ever after, when she heard the clink of a cowbell in summer, her taste buds watered and her nostrils filled with the scent of freshly ironed laundry—and her heart ached with a sorrow she could not name.

The winter afternoon she'd been invited inside the house, she had tried to think of topics for conversation. Should she compliment Mrs. Wayne on her ironing? Or would that remind her hostess of the difference in their stations, as her mother would say? Should she mention Marshall and how much he was admired? Maybe she should comment on the weather, like the grown-ups did when they couldn't think of anything to say. But there was so much to say to Elizabeth Wayne. Did she know that a pair of wrens returned in the spring to the nest they had built in one of the pecan trees the spring before? Was she aware that a fat old bullsnake lived in a camouflaged burrow at the edge of the cornfield? Maybe she ought to be told that a wasp nest was tucked beneath the eave by the front porch swing. And did she realize that this year Marshall would probably be taller than the corn?

But when time came to speak, she had blurted out, "God, I love this place."

Elizabeth had glanced up from the ironing board, her gentle eyes expressing humor and surprise. "Why, whatever would make you say that? We live very simply here."

"No," she had disputed. "It's grand. You live very… grandly."

"Grandly?" Elizabeth had puzzled over the word, thinking no doubt of the splendid house where Aly lived and wondering at the child's meaning. "No, not grandly, child, but we live very happily here."

"Isn't that living grandly?" Aly had wanted to know.

"Marshall is in his room," Elizabeth said when Aly arrived at Cedar Hill the day Willy left. "He's studying for a few hours before he has to go down to the barn to help Sy inventory the equipment. Willy's down there now. He'll stay with us while he's looking for a job. Just go on down and knock on Marshall's door."

"You mean—his bedroom door?" The idea of entering the sanctum of Marshall's room was stupendous to her. She had never had so much as a glimpse into it.

Elizabeth smiled and some of the sparkle returned to her worried eyes. She had long perceived Aly's secret infatuation with her son. "Yes. You impressed him yesterday. He'll be glad to see you."

Aly walked down the breezeway to the second room from the end and knocked on the door. "Come in," Marshall called, his deepened voice carrying authority, confidence. Put off by it, Aly hesitated, then opened the door and entered.

Marshall sat over his books with his back to her, and Aly had a few seconds to run her eye hurriedly over the room where Marshall had grown up. It was a boy's haven, too juvenile now for the full-grown man. Open shelves held an accumulation of athletic equipment from the sports of years past: football, baseball, tennis. Others contained well-thumbed books, mostly paperback, and Aly saw that Edgar Rice Burroughs had been a favorite. One shelf had been devoted entirely to trophies and awards, many of them scholastic. Other memorabilia—pennants, citations, athletic letters—had been tacked on the wall above the twin-sized bed, too short for him now. Aly could imagine his feet hanging off the bed, his dark hair tousled on the pillow...There was also a collection of photographs. Something inside her wrenched painfully as she noted several of her beautiful sister, Victoria. "Hi," she said brightly.

Marshall swung around sharply, obviously having expected his mother. "What do you want?" he demanded, almost rudely. She had disturbed his concentration, she understood at once, hurt scoring her feelings. *Why do I care so much for him?* she wondered. *I can count on one hand the number of smiles I've had from him through the years. Why can't I stop loving him? Why can't I tell him to go to the devil?*

"I—I have an offer to make you," she stammered, appalled that she made it sound like a favor she was asking. She blinked at the rise of tears, refusing to let them come.

At once Marshall's chair scraped back on the hardwood floor. "Hey, Aly," he said tenderly, as she'd once heard him speak to an injured dog found under the house, "don't mind me. I'm sorry for snapping. I've got a lot on my mind right now." He put a hand on her shoulder. "What can I do for you?"

She said without preamble, "I want to buy Sampson for a better price than Matt Taylor is offering. I know how much you love that horse, Marshall. I can keep him for you until you can afford to buy him back. The money will help your family…"

The hand was taken away. Aly could not read the unfathomable dark eyes, but she could feel him wanting to say no. He would be beholden to no Kingston. She braved a hand on his arm. "Please, Marshall. Please let me do this for you."

Her hand dropped as Marshall sighed and tucked his fingers into the tops of his jean pockets. "And what would you do with Sampson once you bought him? Do you know anything about horses?"

"No, but I can learn. I'll find someone who can teach me about them. I would take the best care of him, Marshall, honest. And when you get on your feet financially, you can buy him back from me. I won't ask a cent more than what I bought him for."

"And how much is that?"

"Ten thousand dollars."

Now the dark eyes showed expression. Marshall whistled at the sum. "Ten thousand dollars? Are you kidding? Where would you get that kind of money?"

"From an inheritance I'll be coming into when I'm twenty-four. My dad has agreed to let me borrow against it."

"To buy Sampson? How'd you manage that?"

Aly shrugged and said cockily, "I gave him the old proverbial offer he couldn't refuse."

Marshall laughed, showing his straight white teeth, and sat down on the edge of his desk, bringing himself eye-level with her. "I'll bet you did. But why, Aly? Why do you care so much? God knows, I haven't done anything to deserve your affection. Have my folks meant that much to you?"

"Yes," she answered simply, accepting that Marshall could never appreciate how much she loved his parents and Cedar Hill. He saw this house and Elizabeth and Sy differently than she did. He could never have understood, even if she'd been able to explain, that she respected his parents' failures more than she did her family's successes, that the warm treasures of this house impressed her more than the cold opulence of her own. Here she had found love and acceptance and understanding. Here she had been praised and encouraged and comforted. To think of Cedar Hill in the hands of someone else was ghastly enough, but to think of the Waynes gone from Claiborne was unimaginably worse. If Marshall agreed to her offer, at least she would have a guarantee of seeing him again. Sampson would keep him in her life, give her an excuse to call and write to him occasionally.

"Please, Marshall," she said again. "Please let me buy Sampson from you."

Marshall, with an unexpectedly tender look, reached out and tucked aside her shaggy bangs. "I appreciate your offer, Aly. Believe me I do, but where would you keep Sampson? And besides, you'll be leaving for college in the fall, and who would look after him then?"

"I'm not going to college, Marshall. I don't know yet what I plan to do, but I'm not going to school."

"Your father will make you go. Can you imagine a Kingston not going to college? And there's the problem of a place for Sampson...."

"I'll keep him at one of the riding stables in town. I'll rent a stall and exercise him every day—"

"No, Aly. The answer is no." Marshall stood up with finality. "I can't let you take on a responsibility like Sampson because you feel you have to make up for what your father has done. You're still growing, still changing, and what you feel today won't necessarily be the way you feel tomorrow. A horse is a handful. You don't even know how to ride...."

"Listen to me, Marshall Wayne." Aly's eyes narrowed sternly. "I don't give my word lightly. If I say I'll take care of that horse, I'll take care of him. If I promise to sell him back to you, then I will. I'm your only chance to get Sampson back, and you don't have any right to turn down ten thousand dollars, not with the pickle your family's in. Besides, Willy will be around..."

"Not necessarily, not if he can't get a job in Claiborne, and he won't go near Sampson anyway," Marshall cut in, but Aly could see he was beginning to weaken.

"We're not talking about a lifetime of care, for Pete's sake," she pointed out. "You'll be buying him back within a year!" *Hopefully not*, Aly thought to herself, but she needed all the bait she could get on the hook.

"All right," Marshall conceded, "here's the deal. If you can find a place to stable him that meets with my approval, learn to ride so that you can exercise him, and promise to sell him back to me, we can do business. But," he cautioned, holding up a warning hand to check the burst of delight lighting her face, "I have to know about the stable arrangements today, and no later. I promised Matt I'd let him have my decision about Sampson before I leave in the morning."

"You got it!" Aly exclaimed happily, her features fully aglow now. "You won't ever have any regrets, Marshall."

"I don't think so, either." He laughed with her, and for a second he had been startled by the brief flash of a deep, hidden, totally unexpected beauty.

Propped against the hood of the sports car, the Kingstons' former chauffeur and handyman was waiting for her when she went running down the steps. "Willy!" she cried, throwing her arms around the diminutive man whose left foot stuck out at a crazy angle. His complexion had the smooth look of worn leather, and his round button eyes were as black and endearing as a teddy bear's. "Annie Jo and I are going to miss you so much!"

"I will you two also, Punkin. You know why I left?"

Aly nodded, wondering what resources she could call on for Willy. "You have any plans? What are you going to do?"

"I don't know yet. I'm too small and crippled to work in the oil fields, and I know better than to try to get any other kind of work around here. Everybody in town is in hock to your dad, one way or the other. I'm sure he'll spread the word that I'm poison. I may mosey down to Texas once I've finished up around here."

"Don't despair, Willy. I'll think of something."

He grinned in appreciation and cuffed her chin. "You will too, no doubt. But if I go, I won't leave without saying good-bye or telling you where I can be reached if you ever need me."

Good ol' Dad has really gummed up some lives, Aly thought bitterly as she drove out of the yard.

Chapter Four

Driving toward Claiborne past the gently rolling farmland that made up Cedar Hill, Aly's mind turned to Willy. It was so sad. He had thought he had a home with her parents for the rest of his life. He'd not been paid high wages, but his salary included a comfortable, roomy apartment over the garage and free board, if Annie Jo's meals could be counted as a fringe benefit.

A former jockey, Willy had suffered a shattered hip when his horse had fallen during a race. After release from the hospital, he left the Kentucky bluegrass country of his birth and followed a string of odd jobs down into the flat plains of Oklahoma. He'd avoided horses ever after, not because he held his injuries against them, but because he could never ride again. "Me working around horses would be like an alcoholic working in a liquor store," he once explained to Aly. "Too much pain, too many memories."

He had come to them the month she was born. Her father had hired him to be on hand to drive her mother to the hospital in case he wasn't around. He hadn't been, and Willy had been the one careening around corners and running red lights in the wee hours of the morning to get her mother to the emergency entrance in time for delivery. Annie Jo and Willy had been the first to wave and smile at her through the nursery room glass, and so it had been ever since. They were always the ones to whom she took her triumphs and tragedies.

Well, she thought, at least at Cedar Hill Willy had a home for a while. Once she found a place for Sampson, she would concentrate on one for Willy.

Several hours later, Aly sat seething behind the wheel of her sports car parked in front of the Newton Riding Stable. She'd just been informed by the owner that he had no room to stable another horse, even though Aly had spied two empty stalls with blank nameplates. "What about those?" she had asked, pointing to the end of the stable.

"They're reserved for two boarders coming in at the end of the week."

"Which boarders?"

"That's none of your business, young lady."

"My father put you up to this, didn't he? He called you and warned you that I'd be out, looking for a place to keep Sampson. You're afraid that the bank will call in your loan if you rent a stall to me, aren't you?"

The nervous shift of the stable owner's eyes confirmed to Aly that she had correctly appraised the situation. She'd had the same experience at the other stable.

Now what was she to do? Where could she go for stable space? Which farmer or rancher was not in hock to the Kingston State Bank? The only resident she could think of was Matt Taylor, still referred to as the Connecticut Yankee even though he had come down from New England a quarter of a century before. Hardworking, frugal, and solvent, he owned Green Meadows, one of the finest horsebreeding farms in the state and a neighbor to Cedar Hill. Money changed hands between him and her father because the profits from the farm were deposited in the Kingston State Bank and the bank paid Matt interest on them.

But Matt was bidding for Sampson. Why would he want to rent a stall to her when he found out that she, too, had made an offer for the horse. He would be sure to figure out that the sale was contingent on her securing space for him. Aly put the sports car in reverse gear. Right now she had no other choice but to sound Matt out about it. The worst he could say was no. Dadblameit! She knew the reason for her father's interference. It wasn't the loan. He wanted nothing to prevent her going to college. Aly would have preferred his usual indifference. She'd had more experience with it and had learned how to deal with the pain.

She found Matt in his office, a spacious, comfortable room with large plate glass windows overlooking barns, stables, paddocks, and grazing fields. Green Meadows had produced a number of racing champions, and its stock was noted to be sound, sturdy, and healthy. Aly respected and liked Matt Taylor, a heavy-set man in his early forties who was never too busy to play host to schoolchildren on field trips.

The breeder had never lost his Eastern accent, and his quick clear speech with the hard consonants fell sharply on Oklahoma ears. When she arrived, he was shouting into the phone. "You can tell Benjy Carter that I have no intention of bailing him out of jail on this drunken charge, not this time! You can tell him for me, his former employer, that he can rot in there for all I care." He banged down the phone and scowled at Aly.

"Benjy Carter at it again, Mr. Taylor?"

"Got picked up driving on the wrong side of the road out of Claiborne loop-legged drunk. I've had it with the boy, even though it means I'll be shorthanded until I can find somebody reliable to replace him. That'll be hard to do what with the oil companies siphoning off all the good help these days. What can I do for you, Aly?"

"I'd like to rent a stall from you for a horse I want to buy."

Matt's broad brow furrowed like a newly sown cornfield. "Why, Aly, I'm not in the stall-renting business. You're buying a horse? What kind and who from?" His surprised tone suggested disappointment that she was not buying from him.

Aly sighed. "I was afraid you'd ask me that. I might as well level with you. I want to buy Sampson, Mr. Taylor. Marshall leaves to go back to Pennsylvania tomorrow, and I have to find a place for Sampson by then or he won't sell to me. He'll...sell to you. I've tried both stables, but they're full."

"You must be offering him considerably more than I am."

"I am."

"Well, now," Matt stroked his chin thoughtfully. "I got to say, Aly, that helping you means cutting myself out of a good piece of horseflesh, and I don't see how I can do that. Fact is, knowing how much Marshall loves that horse, I'm surprised he'd even think of selling him to you, not because you're a Kingston, mind you, but because you've never been known to have anything to do with horses. You'll be going off to school in the fall, won't you?"

"No, Mr. Taylor, I won't. I intend to get a job here in Claiborne if I can. And believe me, I've heard all the arguments about why I wouldn't be a good owner for Sampson, but I will be."

Matt looked at her with compassion. "A job, Aly? In this town? It's no secret how your dad feels about your going to school. Who's going to give you a job that would thwart his wishes?"

Aly stared at him. An idea had just popped into her head. "How about you? You're not afraid of Dad's clout, and you're shorthanded, right? You need somebody to take Benjy Carter's place, right? How about me?"

"How about you?" Matt chortled. "Why, you don't know the first things about mucking out stalls and taking care of horses!"

"Mr. Taylor, I can learn." Aly's hazel eyes deepened in earnestness. "I'm a good worker and as reliable as they come. Ask anybody. And—and—you can hire me pretty cheap."

The last piqued Matt's Yankee frugality. He squinted at her closely. "How cheap?"

Aly thought carefully. "For Sampson's room and board," she said slowly, "I'll come out here every morning and work until noon. The rest of the day my services will cost you minimum wage."

"You've got to be out of your mind, young lady. Nobody works for wages like those!"

"I will," Aly said emphatically, beginning to have hope that she had made a deal. "Working here will give me a chance to learn about horses. I've always been curious about them. And you'll be pleased with the quality of my work. I'm sure of it."

Matt Taylor walked over to one of the windows to think over her offer. Aly tried to guess what he was thinking. Was he worried that she'd be too slight to handle the chores or too scared of the horses?

"Tell you what," Aly said, "if you'll agree to my terms, after a month if you're not satisfied with my work, I'll sell Sampson to you for the price you would have paid—six thousand dollars."

Matt's mouth hung open. "You mean you'd lose the difference between what you paid and what I offered?"

"That's right."

"And you'd trust my evaluation of your work?"

"You're known as an honest man, Mr. Taylor. I know you'll deal fairly with me."

"Mucking out stalls is hard, dirty work. What if you don't like it and just decide to quit?"

"Then you'd have another reason Sampson would become yours."

Matt Taylor smiled and held out his hand. "Folks who work at Green Meadows call me Matt," he said. "When can you start?"

The bargain struck, Aly drove out to Cedar Hill to inform Marshall that Sampson had a new home. She found man and horse in the barn and paused just inside the door, reluctant to interrupt the last moments between them. They were in deep conversation—Marshall talking in low tones and Sampson occasionally responding with a soft whinny.

What a wrench it had been for both of them when Marshall had left for college. The stallion had refused to eat for several days and remained listless and despondent for weeks afterward. At Christmas, they'd had a glorious two weeks together before Marshall had to leave again, and once more Sampson pined.

"It happens that way sometimes with unweaned foals," Willy explained, referring to the spindly-legged, malnourished little colt that Sampson had been when Marshall bought him. Rejected by his mother and neglected by his busy owner, the little fellow was slowly dying of starvation when Marshall heard of his plight.

Marshall had gone to the owner and offered the only thing of value he owned in exchange for the colt—a prized flintlock gun left him by his grandfather. The owner had agreed to the trade, and Sampson had gone to live at Cedar Hill, where he and Marshall became all but inseparable. Now after six years, Sampson was to have a new home for a while, his master was explaining, but he'd come for him as soon as he could.

"Marshall?" Aly called softly.

Both master and horse looked in her direction, their eyes

grave and unwelcoming. Feeling an intruder, she said kindly, "I have a place for him."

"Where?" he asked shortly, but Aly knew that pain made him brusque.

"At Matt Taylor's. He's agreed to let me keep Sampson at Green Meadows."

"At Green Meadows?" Marshall said in surprise. "How did you swing that?"

Aly shrugged, smiling slightly. "Offered him one of my special deals. Now how about us? Do we have one?"

Intrigued, Marshall came close to her, one corner of his mouth lifting in a grin. "We do," he said. "Let's shake on it." When Aly gave him her hand, he laughed. "Come on, Aly. How'd you do it? How did you get Matt to agree to board Sampson?"

"I never give out trade secrets, Marshall," she replied, liking the strong but sensitive feel of his hand. *No use telling him about the bargain between Matt and me*, she thought. She was confident that her labor at Green Meadows would be beyond reproach. Sampson was in no danger of being lost because of shabby work. She planned to make herself indispensable.

Marshall's brown eyes glowed in admiration. Aly knew he was relieved that Sampson would have such a good home. "You are something very special, Alyson Kingston," he said approvingly. "Why haven't I ever noticed before?"

"You never looked," she said with simple candor, hoping that now that he was, her freckles weren't standing out like copper pennies. At least she had gone home and changed, not wanting to make her father any madder than he already was when she went to the bank. At home she'd also trimmed her bangs and applied a light touch of makeup. "But then," she added hastily, "there's not much to see."

"There's plenty to see. But *you* have to see it first, Aly. Then make the most of it."

"I wouldn't know how to do either one—"

"Get Victoria to help you."

"I wouldn't give her the satisfaction!" Aly said, suddenly angry. How did this conversation get turned around to Victoria! She realized he was still holding her hand. He held it firmly when she tugged at it.

"Hey," he said mollifyingly, "don't get your dander up. It was just a suggestion." He released her hand. Aly thrust both of hers into the pockets of her skirt.

"Okay, so we have a deal," she said. "I'll leave Sampson here until after the auction."

"Aly, you can change your mind, you know." Her heart began to beat faster as Marshall stepped closer. His voice was quiet and gentle. "You don't owe us anything. You're not responsible for what your father does."

"I know that," she said, lifting her gaze upward. They were almost touching. Aly felt suddenly enclosed with him in a special, very private place, just the two of them and Sampson. "It's just that I—I may never have another opportunity to do anything for your family, Marshall. They mean the world to me, you know. And besides, I'm not buying Sampson for keeps. I expect you to buy him back from me, remember." She smiled at him, and once again her face underwent a startling transformation.

Marshall caught her to him, taking her breath away. "Thanks, Aly," he whispered gratefully. "Thanks for everything. Sampson will be all I have left of Cedar Hill."

Her eyes shut and stinging, her throat hurting, she pushed her face into the hard comfort of his shoulder, thinking, *No, Marshall, I am what you have left of Cedar Hill. I have it all inside of me for safekeeping, all the memories of all the years.* Slipping her arms around his waist, they stayed clasped in friendship and mutual loss for several minutes before Marshall extricated himself and sealed their new bond with a kiss on her forehead. "When I come back for the auction, I'll teach you how to ride Sampson," he promised. "In the meantime, you two can become friends."

"Oh, Marshall, I can hardly wait!" Aly said, beaming. "I'm going by the bank now to pick up the check and sign the loan papers. When are you leaving in the morning?"

"Before daybreak. You want us to meet in town some-where—"

"No, I'll bring the check back out here. I have some things of Willy's to bring him anyway."

"Good," Marshall said. "I'll have the sale agreement ready. Come for supper. Mother's having fried chicken."

"Oh, yum!" Aly said, enormously happy. She gave him a smile. "See you tonight."

At the bank, her father's displeasure had transformed into grudging admiration. *How the devil had she managed to talk Matt Taylor into keeping Sampson on his place? Had she agreed to rent the horse for stud service? What deal had she made?* He bombarded her with questions as Aly followed him into his office.

"None of your business," she answered. "And I think it was pretty low of you to use the bank as a means to keep the other stables from renting to me. However, I must say, things have worked out for the best." She looked infuriatingly pleased with herself, a front assumed to needle her father. Behind the cheerfulness lay the worry that he might find out about her agreement with Matt and somehow wreck it. He was capable of that.

"It was for your own good," her father said, taking a seat at his desk. The paperwork for the money borrowed from her inheritance along with the check for ten thousand dollars were in a file folder on the desk. "That horse will be an enormous liability and will keep you tied down. It will further influence you not to go to college in the fall. I don't care where, as long as you go. Your argument that you have no interests or goals at this point doesn't matter. Your sister didn't either when she went to college."

"She still doesn't, as I see it. Majoring in sorority is not my idea of pursuing a goal."

"Your sister will be graduating with a degree in elementary education!" Lorne stormed, anger making his fine gray eyes icy.

"*If* she doesn't fail one more course," Aly corrected mildly. "If her grades are any reflection of the kind of teacher she'll be, I wouldn't want my kid in her class."

"Young lady—" In frustration Lorne Senior adopted what Aly called his lecture pose: elbows at right angles on the desk, fingers laced tightly, eyes penetrating over the top of his glasses. "Your problem is that you're jealous of your brother and sister. They know where they're going. They've taken steps to provide for their future. You should go and do likewise, rather than stay in Claiborne mooching off your parents until you come into your inheritance."

"I don't have to go to college to find myself. All I have to do is put my right hand on my left elbow, and my left hand on my right elbow," Aly demonstrated, "and I have found myself. And starting tomorrow morning I won't have to mooch off you and Mom anymore, Dad. I've got a job. I'll pay you rent for my room."

Lorne drew back in sharp surprise. "A job? Where?"

"At Green Meadows."

Perplexity gave way to gradual comprehension, clearing Lorne's expression. "So that's how you got Sampson a stall. I heard at Willard's this noon that Benjy Carter got canned because of another DWI charge. You got his job, didn't you? But why would Matt hire you?"

Aly changed the subject. "Have you had the paperwork for the loan drawn up? Is that it on your desk?" She snatched it up before he could grab it. Opening the folder, Aly read the contents and said, "Very good. Give me a pen and I'll sign."

"You're making a mistake doing this, Aly," Lorne pronounced heavily as she signed her name.

"Doing what?" she asked. "Borrowing against my inheritance or not going to college."

"Both."

"Well now, Dad," Aly returned the pen to its holder, "the first mistake I could avoid if you denied me the loan of my money. As trustee, you can do that. But that move would cost the bank several million dollars once I turned twenty-four. A sacrifice that, as president, you're not willing to make to save me from myself. So you can imagine what I think of your concern on that point. And as for going to college, I'm not at all sure that you and Mom want me to go for my benefit or for the sake of family appearances."

"There has never been a Kingston who did not go to college."

"Well, Dad, I am not a typical Kingston." Aly picked up the check and left her father sitting at his desk, his face set in grim acceptance of that fact. After a moment of staring at the closed door, he lifted the phone.

Aly left the bank, aching from the emptiness that always followed a bitter session with her father. It was true what she had said. She entertained no illusions about her place in the family. She knew that she was the child who never should have been. Before her birth, the family was complete. Her parents had the only children they wanted, a son and daughter who were perfect replicas of themselves.

"They say," her mother had said to the rest of the family peering down at the infant in its bassinet—or so Annie Jo had related years later—"that if a baby is ugly at birth, it grows up to be beautiful. Let's hope so."

But she had not grown up to be beautiful nor even to own a redeemable temperament. Furthermore, her concept of the family's position in Claiborne differed considerably from that of the other Kingstons.

"Alyson, you are absolutely *not* to play with Wade Conners, you understand? We have certain standards to maintain in Claiborne, and Wade Conners doesn't meet them. He is totally unsuitable company for the daughter of a bank president. You are not to invite him to this house ever again."

"But why not, Mother? He's funny and he makes me laugh."

"He's unclean and he smells bad. You could catch something from him."

"His mother is dead and his father is a drunk. He takes care of himself the best way he can."

"Really, Alyson," Victoria chimed in, "why do you play with such creatures!"

"Because they like me the way I am."

In grade school she built a playhouse next to the fence in the alley, and from there, fed all the stray dogs and cats that came to her door. It was there she entertained the Wade Connerses of her acquaintance, sneaking them in through the back door of her family's grand home when a bathroom was required. After a while she came to be called Aly, a nickname appropriate to her nonfamily connections and one that could fortunately be explained as a shortened version of her name. Only her mother called her Alyson and would have loved her, Aly knew, if she had not proved to be a book too complicated to read. In time she was set aside and rarely picked up again. Aly watched as her mother turned her time, energy, and hopes to her other, less provocative children. But her father, a perceptive, astute man, was a different matter. As Aly drove out to Cedar Hill, she was thinking that he read her with perfect understanding and disapproved of the text.

Chapter Five

All right, young lady, I've assigned you to Joe Handlin here. He's our stable manager, and you'll be taking your orders from him." Matt Taylor indicated a tall, rangy young man Aly guessed to be in his early twenties. He also looked vaguely familiar. His hair—what could be seen of it below a battered cap bearing the logo of Green Meadows—was the reddish brown hue of the large round freckles dotting his friendly countenance. "Joe, this is Aly Kingston. She's taking Benjy's place, as I told you. You're supposed to teach her everything you know about running the stables."

The other eight members of the staff, gathered for a quick Monday meeting in Matt's office, looked on in amusement as Joe stuck out a large, freckled hand. "Lord have mercy, Matt—in just a week?"

Aly looked puzzled. "A week? Are you going somewhere?"

"No, but you are." Joe grinned amicably. The eyes, Aly could see, were not friendly at all. "I figure a week of the kind of work you'll be doing will just about do it before we see the last of you and that little sports car out there."

So that was it, thought Aly in quick understanding. She glanced quickly at Matt, wondering if he had apprised his manager of their bargain. Reading her query, the breeder shook his head almost imperceptibly. Aly withdrew her hand and gave Joe an unperturbed smile. "Don't place any bets on it," she said.

The meeting over, Aly followed Joe out to the large complex of stables and listened carefully as he explained her main responsibilities. She had already gathered from Matt's briefing that the busiest time of the breeding season was over and now the staff was mainly engaged in taking care of the pregnant mares, supervising the foaling, and caring for the newborns.

"You can rest easy if you're worried about having anything to do with the breeding operation," Joe explained. "That's left for the experienced horsemen. What you'll be doing is mucking out stalls, grooming, watering, and feeding the horses. It's a full-time, never-ending job, with no glory to it and little reward except knowing that the finest four-legged creatures on God's earth have good food, fresh water, and clean stalls. If I ever find a horse in your care lacking any of the three, you can bet I'll ask Matt to can you. Benjy may be a drunk, but I could count on his affection for horses. I don't know that I can yours. Matt tells me you barely know one end of a horse from the other. That so, Miss Kingston?"

"That's so, Joe," Aly puffed, nearly having to run to keep up with him. "But I'm a fast learner and a hard worker. Please call me Aly."

"I call only my friends by their first names, Miss Kingston." Joe pushed open both halves of a wide Dutch door and entered a large barn. Aly, her cheeks warm from the rebuff, followed Joe's rangy figure down an immaculate concrete corridor to a small glass-enclosed office on the right. Joe stepped inside and pushed a button. Instantly soft music flooded the barn and equine heads began to appear over the tops of stall doors.

"Horses like music," he explained, going back to the first stall. The quarterhorse inside was wide awake and happy to see

Joe. She nuzzled Joe's shirt pocket as he slid his hand along the well-muscled neck. "Don't have no sugar for you this morning, sweetheart," he said. "I brought you something else this morning. Come over here, Miss Kingston, and meet Lady Loverly."

Aly obeyed. The horse's abdomen was huge. "Why," she exclaimed, glancing at the swollen udders, "she's expecting!"

Joe glanced at her in surprise. "She sure is. How'd you know?"

"Women know these things, Mr. Handlin," Aly said loftily, stressing the last name and deciding not to confess that she had stayed up way past midnight reading a book that Marshall had given her. "When will she foal?"

"In about a month. In the meantime, we have to keep her away from the stallions. Should one cover her"—Aly could guess what that meant—"Lady Loverly would most likely abort, and we would lose a valuable foal, not to mention what might happen to my sweetheart here." He patted the chestnut neck one last time and moved on to the next stall, explaining that the first thing he did "of a morning" was to go into each horse's stall and check him or her all over—"to make sure nothing has happened during the night."

"Like what?" asked Aly.

"Well, the horse could have injured itself in some way or become sick. And of course with the mares, there's always a slim chance of a miscarriage."

Aly watched Joe lift the white-socked foot of a Thoroughbred stallion and examine the hoof closely. She could come to like Joe, but it was plain he had reservations about her. She suspected the reason had to do with her last name. She asked suddenly, "Weren't you a classmate of my sister?"

Joe raised up and placed his hand at the base of the Thoroughbred's ear. "Feel right here," he ordered.

Aly placed her hand where his had been. "It's warm," she said.

"It should be. Anytime that area feels cool, it's a symptom of a temperature. Horses can't talk, you know. They can't let you know that they have a pulled muscle or a toothache or an upset stomach. You have to look for the symptoms that indicate their problems."

"But didn't you two date for a while?" Aly persisted as they moved to the next stall.

Joe did not look at her. "I wouldn't say that we dated. When she was a sophomore, I took her out a couple of times, that's all. I was a senior then."

Now Aly remembered the gawky, carrot-topped boy that Victoria had kept waiting in the uncomfortable elegance of the Kingston living room. Awkward and self-conscious, in jeans too short for his lanky height, he had stood first on one foot and then the other as he'd tried to make conversation with Eleanor—as out of place in such surroundings as he was in Victoria's love life. Aly had wondered at the time what her sister was up to.

As if recalling the same memory, Joe fastened a hand on the stall door and turned to her, his light green eyes silvering with the remembered humiliation. "Your sister got me to go out with her as part of a hazing routine when she pledged the Cotillion Club. I didn't know that, of course. I should have suspected something when the prettiest girl in school came on to me out of the blue. But I didn't. After two dates, when her quest was completed," Joe spit out the words, "she brushed me off quicker'n you would a red ant." He barked a laugh, the eyes glittering. "You Kingstons aren't noted for the way you handle folks. Or maybe you are, come to think of it. I hear your old man just foreclosed on the Wayne farm. That so?"

"Yes," Aly answered stiffly, embarrassed and feeling the helpless anger that always afflicted her when she encountered people hurt by members of her family. She pulled at the stall door, but Joe held it shut. Apprehensively, she glanced up at the hostile face.

"Then you better hear this, Miss Kingston. I don't know what you're doing out here, or what your old man has on Matt that would force him to hire you, but horses ain't like people who can be played with and dropped when you lose interest. Thursday is my one day off a week. If I come back out here on Friday morning and find that my horses haven't been properly cared for, I'll give you a thrashing you'll never forget. I don't give a damn if you are a Kingston. I'll take my chances with your old man when I get through with you. You got that?"

"I got it," said Aly. "Now we better check on—" she glanced down at the name printed on the white card in the nameplate. "Old MacDonald here. He has a runny nose. Isn't that a sign of congestion?"

At six o'clock when her day was finished, Aly's fatigue was matched only by her elation. *I could really get into this!* she decided on the way out to Cedar Hill. Tonight when she returned home, she would stop by the public library before closing time and check out some books on the breeding of horses.

Elizabeth, to stave off the loneliness of Marshall's departure, had asked that she have supper with them again, and Aly, her mouth watering from the smell of roast pork and dressing, was ready to faint from hunger by the time she sat down at the sumptuously laden table on the screened-in back porch.

"Aly," Elizabeth said firmly as she heaped a plate for her guest, "you'll have to start eating more if you're to do a man's work for Matt Taylor."

"I know," said Aly, her mouth full of the succulent tender meat, "but I can't seem to get down anybody's food but yours."

"Then you'll just have to start taking your meals with us."

Aly stared at Elizabeth. Willy and Sy looked up, too, and all eating momentarily halted. "Why don't you stay with us until the farm is sold?" Elizabeth suggested. "I've talked Sy into staying until then. No point in leaving my garden to die. We'll stay until someone else takes over. You're welcome to live with us until then." She passed some more gravy down to Aly, pretending not to notice the surprise of her listeners. "You've always loved this house. There isn't too much time left to enjoy it. I'd like for you to stay with us, Aly. Besides," she added, her smile fond, "how else can I teach you how to cook?"

"Elizabeth...Sy...," Aly looked from one to the other, reading the hope of her acceptance on both their faces. Willy winked at her, the black eyes hopeful. "I'd love to," she said. "Oh, how much I'd love to."

Over her parents' indignant protests, Aly moved out of the family home on Elm Drive out to Cedar Hill, where she was given a simple, spare, but immaculate room next to Marshall's. At the end of the first week, weary but contented, Aly lay awake in her room thinking of the new direction her life was taking. She was finding to her great amazement that she loved being around horses and the men who worked with them. It was a frank, forthright kind of labor that suited her own direct manner and straightforward nature. She had made mistakes this week, but they had been forgiven as honest ones, and she was certain that at the end of the month, Sampson could be declared rightfully hers.

By then, both Marshall and Victoria would be home—Marshall for the auction and Victoria for the summer. Her older sister had already accepted a teaching job in Oklahoma City.

Aly thought of the pictures hanging on the wall in the next room. Did Marshall care for Victoria? Had all these years of indifference toward her been a façade to protect his pride from the ruthlessness of her beauty. Had he deliberately avoided the trap into which poor Joe Handlin had fallen? She knew Victoria had always had a hankering for Marshall. But for what, for how long, was anybody's guess.

In the following days, Sy looked for work at the surrounding ranches and farms. Nobody was hiring except the oil companies, and Elizabeth drew the line at her husband going near a dangerous drilling rig, even if he'd been qualified. Each night at the supper table, he seemed more drawn and depressed, his spirits not lifting even when he and Willy sat down to play dominoes.

Aly went with Elizabeth in search of a place to live once the farmhouse reverted to other hands. Never before had Aly realized how short of rental property Claiborne was. Every available accommodation had been snapped up by oil-field workers, and Aly was surprised that her father had not taken advantage of the situation by building apartment houses.

"Marshall wants us to come up to New York to live with him," Elizabeth confided, "but Sy won't hear of it. We'd be lost in the city. What would we do with ourselves while Marshall is at work? And he doesn't need us on his hands, not with all the mountains that son of mine intends to climb."

At night, lying in her bed, Aly beseeched heaven to assist her in finding a way to help the Waynes and Willy. For fear of asking for too many miracles, she did not ask to be granted Marshall's love. She would settle for friendship, more miracle than she had ever hoped for. She was counting the days when he would be home to teach her how to ride Sampson.

She was learning how to cook, and each day she looked forward to the meal she would help Elizabeth prepare that night. "My jeans have shrunk!" she wailed one morning as she sat down to breakfast.

Elizabeth suppressed a smile. "Have they now?" she said, sliding a thick slice of ham onto Aly's plate. "Have you weighed yourself lately?"

Later that morning, Aly stepped on the scales in the birthing barn where newborn foals were weighed. Her mouth dropped open. She had gained five pounds while living with the Waynes! That evening, naked, she inspected herself in the full-length mirror attached to her closet door. The hollows of her collarbone and pelvis seemed less prominent, her hips and breasts a trifle fuller. Was it possible, Aly speculated, that only a few pounds more would give her a tolerable figure?

"You know, you remind me of a girl I went to school with," Elizabeth said one evening when Marshall was three days away from coming home. They were on the back porch shelling pecans gathered from the fall bounty of the two trees·in the front yard.

"How's that?" Aly asked, her mind on the sad question of who would be gathering the nuts next year.

"She was awfully plain." Aly's head popped up, but Elizabeth went on with her story. "When we were seniors, our gym instructor predicted the futures of all of us girls, and in most cases time has proved her right."

"What did she predict for you?"

"That I would probably marry a farmer and live a hard but happy life, not so surprising since I was engaged to Sy at the time. But it was her prediction for Emmalou Fuller that surprised us the most."

"The plain one, the girl I remind you of?"

Elizabeth nodded, her hands busy with the pecans. "She said

that Emmalou was a late bloomer and would develop into a beautiful woman by her late twenties. Hers, the teacher said, was the kind of beauty that got lovelier with time, like sterling."

Aly's hands were motionless. "Did that happen?"

"Oh, yes. She moved away from Clarksville after we all graduated. Years later I ran into her in Tulsa. I hardly recognized her, she was so beautiful. She was a career woman by then, very fashionable and modern. She was thirty years old."

"So the gym teacher's prediction came true."

"Well." Elizabeth pondered a moment. "I have my own theory about that. Emmalou's beauty was always there, in my opinion, but in her mind she thought herself unattractive and no competition for the other girls she considered so much prettier. She refused to do the best she could with the looks she had— sort of like children who won't play games they cannot win. I don't think Emmalou was exactly a late bloomer. I think she just moved away from an environment where she could not blossom." Elizabeth looked at Aly with affection. "I have a feeling you might be an Emmalou Fuller, child."

Later in her room, Aly ruminated over Emmalou's story, objectively studying herself in the mirror in search of a wealth of hidden beauty that she, too, might possess. Other than clear, nicely shaped hazel eyes and fairly good skin beneath the freckles, she couldn't find much potential for Elizabeth's prediction coming true. And furthermore, there was nowhere she wanted to go "to blossom." It was the darndest thing. Like most of her friends, she ought to be perishing to get away from Claiborne, out from under the critical eyes of her family and the censure of being a Kingston. But she had no desire to leave, not yet. Not until she had a reason. Her father was right, of course. She ought to be thinking about what she intended to do with the rest of her life. But those thoughts could wait another summer, at least until Marshall came home and left again, until she could see how this job with Matt worked out.

"Remember that I won't be having supper here this evening, Elizabeth," Aly said unenthusiastically the next morning. Victoria arrived today, and her mother had called to insist that Aly have dinner with the family. Aly made a face. "Lord only knows what Annie Jo will have us sit down to."

Elizabeth smiled and handed her the sack lunch she prepared daily for her young boarder. "I put in an extra piece of chicken and a slice of cake. That should see you through the day."

At the main barn, Aly saw Joe Handlin's personal car. "Good morning," she said to the stable manager in the stall of Lady Loverly. "What are you doing back out here? Today is Thursday."

Joe was running his hand gently down the swollen sides of the mare. "I'm a little concerned about my sweetheart here. I think she'll foal before the vet thinks she will. She looks mighty uncomfortable to me."

She did to Aly also. The mare's tail twitched restlessly, and her head turned constantly to observe her bulging belly. Aly still found it unbelievable that inside a miniature horse waited to be born. "Do you think she should have exercise today, Joe?"

"Only if she wants to go with you. If she is turned out, for God's sake, make sure Jim Beam's not in the paddock. He has the hots for my sweetheart here. The fact that she's ready to foal won't stop him. Also, get a stall ready for her in the foaling barn just in case. Keep an eye on her udder. If she begins to drip, take her immediately to the foaling barn and call Matt. He'll take over from there."

Joe removed his cap and scratched his carroty head. "I wouldn't take today off at all, but I promised I'd take my aunt into Oklahoma City to shop."

Aly laid a reassuring hand on his arm. "Go ahead and enjoy yourself, Joe. Show Aunt Hattie a good time. I'll see after your old sweetheart here. I'll prepare her a stall fit for a queen. Maybe by the time you get here in the morning, she'll have a surprise for you."

Joe's freckled countenance showed his growing affection for the new stable hand. He had been calling her Aly for over a week now. "I know you'll see after her, Aly. I've come to depend a lot on you." He put his hat back on his head. "See you in the morning."

Aly hurried to feed and water the horses so that she could get over to the foaling barn to prepare a stall for Lady Loverly. The man in charge was on vacation now that nearly all of the pregnant mares had dropped their young. Lady Loverly's delivery was the only one imminent. Working alone, Aly removed all the previous straw and droppings with a pitchfork and wheelbarrow and then swept the floor of the thermostatically controlled stall. After disinfecting it with soap and water, she dusted the concrete with powdery white lime to ensure its cleanliness, then laid a clean dry bed of straw over it. She remembered that Joe had said that it must be deep but not impossible for the foal to move around in. Finally, assured that the stall would meet Joe's expectations, she went back to complete her chores at the other barn.

From time to time during the day, Aly checked on the mare, whose tail continued to twitch fitfully. When Lady Loverly began to pace in her stall, Aly said, "What's wrong, old girl? Tired of your room? Well, come on, and Aly will take you out for your constitutional."

Slipping a halter on the mare, Aly led her to an empty paddock and watched her graze from the fence. It was a perfect June day, peaceful and sunny with small white clouds dotting the clean blue sky. How she loved it here at Green Meadows. She might very well have found her life's work, thanks to her good fortune in buying Sampson, now good friends with his new mistress. After the auction, she and Marshall would bring him out to Green Meadows together. Wouldn't he be surprised to learn that she worked here and had the run of the place!

After a while, deciding that Lady Loverly had taken the air enough, Aly led her back up the bridle path, careful not to jostle her bulging sides. Like Joe, she felt the birth very near. Maybe that excitement or the fact of Marshall's coming home or the simple beauty of the afternoon accounted for the happiness bursting inside her. Not even knowing that Victoria was home for the summer could blight her newfound joy. In her innocence and ignorance of life, she doubted that anything could.

At six o'clock, Aly patted Lady Loverly's neck one last time, reluctant to leave her. The mare was pacing back and forth, back and forth in her stall, stopping at intervals to peer at her heavy sides. If only the family dinner were tomorrow night, she thought, wishing she had the nerve to call and cancel. But Matt was home and a nightwatchman was on duty, though Aly suspected that he slept most of the night. "Now, listen," she instructed the aging groomsman as she was leaving, "you make sure that you check on Lady Loverly constantly during the night. She's expecting, you know, so you hurry up and get Matt if she goes into labor."

As she drove up Elm Drive to her parents' white columned house, Aly suddenly remembered that she'd not had a chance to make herself presentable in any way, not with so many of the men on vacation now that the breeding season was practically over. Oh, well, what did she care? Shame immediately followed the thought. Why did she persist in thumbing her nose at her family and their way of life? Was it because she really wanted to fit in but was afraid she couldn't if she tried? Was she an Emmalou Fuller in that respect, refusing the race because of the competition?

Her guilt was short-lived when her family, gathered for cocktails in the living room, turned shocked heads at her entrance. Aly paused in the doorway, her smile showing first embarrassment, then rebellion. Why did they always see the dirty clothes, the freckles, and lank hair? Why couldn't they ever see *her* and be glad she was there? "Well, howdy, folks," she said in a pronounced Oklahoma twang to annoy her mother. "Just in time for a glass of wine, I see. I can use it. How are you, Victoria? Back for a while? When are you leaving?"

"Young lady!" Eleanor's tone was sharp. She stood up from the couch, looking in a pink summer dress almost as breathtaking as her older daughter. "Go upstairs and wash before you sit down anywhere in this house. Then you may have a glass of wine. I'll tell Annie Jo to hold dinner."

"Well, let me say hello first." Victoria laughed, rising to go to her sister. Holding a glass of sherry in a dainty hand and bending to avoid contact with Aly's clothes, she kissed Aly lightly on the cheek. Aly caught a whiff of fragrance composed of more than Victoria's perfume. It was a compound of fresh glowing skin and silky blond hair and white sparkling teeth—it was the scent of sheer femininity. "How are you, Alyson? I do believe you look happy. Are you?"

"Very," Aly answered, adamantly.

"Well, good for you! I'm happy that you are."

Aly looked narrowly at her sister, suspicious of her sincerity, but the heavily fringed blue eyes gazed back affectionately. That was the trouble with Victoria. Sometimes out of her preoccupation with herself there beamed an unexpected ray of sisterly love. "Hurry upstairs and get back so that we can have time for a drink together before we have to face Annie Jo's efforts," Victoria urged. "I'm eager to hear about your work."

"Okay!" Aly grinned, happy, in spite of knowing she should know better, that Victoria was home.

Meals were served in the Kingston household for the affirmation of the family's status rather than for sustenance. Eleanor had never encouraged Annie Joe to improve her cooking, having discovered certain advantages in serving unappetizing and boring meals. Calories were more easily controlled and table manners taught if family members were disinterested in the food. Conversation could flow between bites, and more attention could be given to the proper use of utensils. Eleanor regarded the genteel clink of sterling against china, of cups returned to porcelain as more satisfying—more appropriate to the kind of people they were—than the sound of a family relishing its food.

"Have you learned to ride yet?" asked Victoria, sawing at a slice of boiled roast.

"No," Aly answered. "When Marshall comes home for the auction, he's supposed to give me some riding lessons on Sampson."

"Is he really?" Victoria's blue eyes widened. "Do you suppose he could teach me, too? I've always wanted to ride. It's such an *in* thing now."

"Then I suggest you take lessons at the riding stable while you're home," Aly replied at once. "Marshall will only be home for a few days. He has a job at one of the biggest banks in New York."

"He'll have time to teach you," Victoria reminded her with a slightly amused look.

"I'm used to horses. You aren't. Marshall won't have time for you to become familiar with them."

"Well, then," said Victoria brightly, "I'll just come out to Green Meadows and watch him teach you."

Under the table, Aly's hand balled into a fist. She did not reply but concentrated on the best way to destring the green beans on her plate, conscious that when Victoria lifted her wineglass, her lips curved into a smile before she drank.

Chapter Six

Driving into the entrance of Green Meadows the next morning, Aly recognized the station wagon of Doc Talley drawn near the foaling barn. She parked hurriedly in front of Matt's office, casting thoughts of Marshall, Victoria, and the auction aside as she ran up the paved walking path between the white-railed paddocks to the barn. Doc Talley was the specialist summoned when a horse developed problems beyond the expertise of the local veterinarian Matt usually used. Aly's heart pounded. Was something wrong with Lady Loverly? Had she foaled during the night and something gone haywire? Joe wasn't due back until the afternoon. How terrible for him to return to find that something had happened to his old sweetheart.

Several trainers and groomsmen were loitering about the doorway of the barn, looking anxious and talking in low tones. "What's the matter?" Aly asked breathlessly, running up to them.

The men broke off their conversation to stare at her in hard-faced silence. "See for yourself," one of them eventually said, jerking his head toward the open doorway.

As she entered the well-lit barn, Aly could smell the sharp, acidulous mixture of sweat and blood. At her feet began a trail of brownish red splotches leading to the birthing stall, next to which was a large black plastic sack, securely tied and labeled. She closed her eyes a moment, dizzy from the odor and the shocking realization of what must have happened. Doc Talley and Matt stood at the open door of the stall, tight-lipped and dour.

Nearing them, Aly quavered, "Matt, is it Lady Loverly?"

They acknowledged her with the same piercing scrutiny she'd received from the other men, and for the first time she realized that they were standing at the stall to the right of the one she had prepared for Lady Loverly. She stared back in confusion. What was going on?

"Yes," Matt glowered. "Didn't you know not to leave a pregnant mare in a meadow where a stallion could get to her, Aly? Jim Beam was in the one where you left Lady Loverly. As a result, she aborted her foal, a little colt that would have been a beauty. Thank God, Joe was worried about her and got back to town early. He came out around ten o'clock and found her gone from her stall."

"Joe was able to get her back here before she foaled," Doc said, adding his own note of censure. "Weren't you supposed to get a stall ready for her?"

"Well, yes. I did—"

"You call that a stall ready for a foaling mare?" Matt demanded, pointing at the stall Aly had cleaned.

She went to peer over its door. The wheelbarrow of soiled hay and droppings had been dumped back on the floor and spread around to indicate that the stall had not been cleaned. "Matt—" she said in dismay, her eyes round with disbelief. "I—I don't know what's going on here. Joe—" She moved between the two men to stare into Lady Loverly's stall. Joe was kneeling beside her, stroking and murmuring words of endearment and comfort. The mare lay very still, the only sign of life the slight rise and fall of her smeared side. "Joe, I didn't leave her in the meadow—"

"Get her out of here, Matt," Joe said without the slightest change of tone. He might have been cooing to Lady Loverly. "Get her out of here before I kill her. I trusted her. I should have known better than to trust a Kingston, but I did, and I nearly lost my ol' sweetheart here."

"No!" Aly gasped the denial, restrained from entering the stall by the two men. "Joe, it isn't true! I never left Lady Loverly in the meadow. She was in the barn when I left yesterday at six. And I left this stall"—she indicated the one she had prepared—"clean and comfortable enough for a baby. Ask the nightwatchman, he'll tell you. I told him to keep an eye on Lady Loverly because she could foal any minute. Ask him!"

Matt sighed heavily. "I did ask him. He said that the mare was still in the meadow when you left early yesterday afternoon." Joe had gotten to his feet, green eyes narrowed to glittering slits. Stains of blood and afterbirth covered his clothes, horrifying evidence of the mare's agony and loss. In a voice still soft so as not to disturb Lady Loverly, he began to call her and her family a string of epithets too profane for her comprehension.

"No!" Aly pleaded, covering her ears. "It's not true. Joe, I never…"

Doc and Matt took her by the arms and hustled her out of earshot of the hair-raising voice. Outside the barn, Matt pushed his cap back and considered her with scowling disappointment. "Aly, I'm surprised at you. I thought you were working out pretty good around here. Of all times to slack off…"

"Matt, listen to me," Aly begged, her freckles standing out like tiny copper discs on her white face. "I didn't slack off. Somebody messed up the stall I had prepared and turned that mare loose after I left here at six o'clock yesterday. The night-watchman was either asleep or lying." A thought struck her. "Wait a minute! Matt, you—you didn't do this to—to get Sampson, did you?"

Shame and regret washed over her the second she'd said it, and she recognized that she'd made a terrible, irrevocable mistake. Matt's lips thinned. His florid cheeks surged with color. "What an outrageous thing to say," he gritted out. "I won't even dignify that question with an answer. For your information, I was on the verge of telling you to forget our deal, that you'd just have to find another place to keep Sampson. But I've changed my mind, young lady. Now you get in your little car and get off my property before Joe comes out of that barn. I'll send you your wages. For Marshall's sake, I'll wait until after the auction, and then I'm going to go pick up that horse. I figure he'll just about make up the difference of what you cost me today."

"You have something to tell me?" Marshall spoke from the doorway of the front parlor where his mother had sent him to find Aly. He felt as if a weight of iron were hanging from his heart. Outside on the lawn, beneath the spreading pecan trees, the auctioneers were setting up their equipment in preparation of selling off an accumulation of a lifetime. Already buyers had begun arriving, parking their pickups and trailers in ready access of the equipment and livestock they hoped to carry off.

His father and Willy were down in the empty barn playing dominoes, seemingly unconcerned about the proceeding that would deprive the Waynes of a means by which to continue the only livelihood they knew. But Marshall, who had just left his red-eyed mother tilling her garden, had seen the vacant look of suffering in the eyes of his father, and a resurgence of hatred burned like a hot flame in his chest.

Looking at the daughter of the man he held responsible for his parents' misery, Marshall made an effort to curb his anger. Aly had nothing to do with this. She had been nothing less than a friend to his family, to him. His mother loved her like a daughter, and the girl, from the look of her, was suffering every bit as deeply as the rest of them. "What is it?" he asked. "Better make it fast, Aly. I still have to tag the items not to be sold."

Aly swallowed with difficulty. She was sitting in rigid composure on the worn Victorian sofa that would soon go to the auctioneer's block. Her face looked pinched and gray. With eyes fixed unseeingly on a view out the window, she said, "I lost Sampson. I had to sell him to Matt Taylor."

"What!" The sound was like an explosion to her ears. "What do you mean you had to sell him to Matt Taylor?" Marshall went to stand in front of her. "Answer me, Aly! Look at me!"

Aly obeyed, lifting eyes hollow with misery. "In order to get a stall for Sampson," she explained haltingly, "I made a deal with Matt that I would work for—for certain wages. If he wasn't satisfied with my work, I—I'd sell him Sampson."

Marshall regarded her in disbelief. "All right. So what happened?"

Aly told him the details as she knew them. Finishing the narrative, she said, "Marshall, I beg you to believe that I didn't turn that mare out like that. I don't know who did, but I didn't."

"Do you really think Matt Taylor capable of such a thing?" he asked tightly, visibly struggling with his anger. His eyes were black and condemning.

Her mouth dry, she said, "No, of course not."

"Then who else would have any motive?"

Aly said nothing. Marshall waited. Finally he said, "This is what I believe. I believe you saw a chance to quit early because Joe was away and couldn't keep an eye on you. Being at your family's dinner party last night was more important than seeing that mare safely stalled. You know so little about horses, I'm sure you didn't realize that she was so close to foaling or that Jim Beam was in the meadow. I'll give you credit for that much. And I guess I should thank you for what you tried to do for me, for my family, but I just can't bring myself to do it, Aly." His mouth twisted in repugnance. "I'd have thought more of you for making no deal at all on our behalf than to make one that was too inconvenient to keep. But I will ask this favor of you. Get out of this house and don't come around while I'm here. I'm sick to death of you Kingstons. I never want to see any of your faces again—not until I'm ready."

As the plane landed, Marshall deliberately remained in his seat and was not deceived by the indifferent glance the woman from the airport cast his way as she stepped into the aisle. He read it as clearly wondering if he were staying on board. Why did she seem so familiar? Again, she seemed to him a little disconcerted, and he was all but convinced that she knew him and had chosen not to acknowledge him. Well, that was not so surprising. Sometimes shy women found him a bit intimidating. He watched her pull on her coat, draw her hair out from under the collar, and stand it close to her face. Her hair shone beneath the lights, soft and bouncy. Intrigued now, he waited for her to leave the plane, then went to stand partially inside the door next to the flight attendant. He smiled and explained, "I just want to see if the young lady with the bouncy blond hair looks back."

When Aly did so, the hostess looked at him with a knowing smile and asked saucily, "Was there any doubt?"

Her heart pounding, Aly hurried into the comparatively quieter atmosphere of the Will Rogers World Airport than the busy Dallas/Fort Worth terminal she had just left, and kept her vision straight ahead. She would not look back to see if Marshall had deboarded. That little trick he had just pulled might have been nothing but outrageous flirtation, something to mollify his ego since she didn't fall all over him in Dallas, but she thought Marshall's ego healthier than that. She had felt his eyes on her all during the flight. Well, what did it matter? If he were coming to Claiborne, he would understand well enough why she'd ignored him. And she could add: *You scared me, Marshall. I remember the way you left, what you thought of us, the promise you made. Now I want to know why you're back.*

But he wasn't coming on to Claiborne. He was staying on the plane, headed for St. Louis. One last furtive look back as she went out the exit did not find him among the group of passengers headed toward the baggage pickup.

She had no luggage to claim. She had gone to Dallas only for the night to purchase a Thoroughbred stallion she'd coveted for Green Meadows for some time. She should have been feeling elated at the acquisition. The addition of the stallion's lineage to her breeding stock would make the farm competitive with the best of the long-established Kentucky operations. But seeing Marshall again had unnerved her. She felt an odd anger and resentment toward him, unsure if she were disappointed or relieved that he was going on to St. Louis.

It was five o'clock. Aly walked to her station wagon in the long-term parking lot, buttoning her coat. The last of winter still gripped the plateau city of Oklahoma City. Red residue of an earlier passing dust storm hung in the sharp cold air and lay in shallow drifts against curbs and tire wheels. Leaving the airport, she glanced in the rearview mirror as if expecting to find a familiar dark head behind the wheel of a rental car.

Feeling foolish, she told herself that even had he gotten off the plane, Marshall would not have had time to take possession of it.

Suppose they had shared a seat on the plane and she had introduced herself, Aly conjectured as she maneuvered the car out into rush-hour traffic. Suppose he had been pleased that they had met again after all these years? What would they have discussed? General news from home, naturally—births, deaths, marriages, and divorces. Claiborne's economy, the drought, the oil bust, wheat prices. She would have deliberately skirted the subjects of Elizabeth's death, Cedar Hill, her father's pending retirement, and her brother's assumption of his title as president and chairman of the Kingston State Bank. But she would have willingly shared news of Willy and Sampson, told Marshall about getting a degree in animal science from the University of Oklahoma—she who had been so opposed to going to college—and about buying Green Meadows from Matt Taylor six years ago when a massive heart attack had forced him to retire.

And Marshall? What would he have offered about himself, his career, his success in New York City? There had been no news at all of him since Elizabeth's burial in the cemetery outside of town. It was only weeks after Marshall had brought his mother's body home that she had learned that he had been in town. The caretaker at the cemetery had told her the news when she went screaming into the little shack that housed his equipment and coffeepot. He'd made her drink a cup of the scalding brew before he relinquished a shred of information about Marshall. "He was a fine sight, he was," the old man said with a note of pride. "Very rich-looking and successful. His folks would have been so proud of him."

Would she have learned that he was married, had children,

possessed a home, a family dog or cat, perhaps another Sampson since he loved horses so? Would he have brought out pictures, smiling with unabashed pride as he indicated the loves and possessions that had finally filled out his life?

Aly didn't think so. For all the successful aura about Marshall Wayne, he didn't look to her the least "filled out." Something was still missing, and she thought it had to do with all those things people take snapshots of and carry around in their wallets. Marshall Wayne was not married now and had never been. A hard little core of certainty told her this was true. She believed she would have known intuitively had he married, just like Elois Cranston had known that her son, days before she got the telegram, had been killed in Vietnam.

Ten miles before reaching the city limit of Claiborne, Aly turned off onto a country road leading to a ranch house. She'd promised the rancher the delivery of two horse blankets when she returned from Dallas, not having had time to stop the afternoon before. He and his wife pressed her to stay for a cup of coffee, and it was close to six-thirty when she once again reached the highway. She stopped to wait for an oncoming car, wondering whether she should mention to her family at dinner tonight that she'd seen Marshall. There was no reason to, she decided, just as the car flashed by.

It was a white Lincoln Continental, a fact that registered only after the identity of the man driving it. The driver was Marshall Wayne, and he was on his way to Claiborne.

Aly sat motionless, possessed by sheer terror for a few moments before reason returned. What was she so fearful of? Most likely this visit had nothing to do with Marshall's threat of thirteen years ago. At thirty-five, Marshall Wayne could very well be at that stage in his life when he felt the need to return to his roots, to go home again. But there, of course, was the rub. There was no home anymore. No farm, no house, no Cedar Hill—not the way he remembered it. She must warn her father. He must be prepared for the possibility of an unpleasant encounter with him. Marshall had rented a white Lincoln Continental. The car could be a simple coincidence or a chilling intimation.

Someday, Aly, my car—my Lincoln—will be in that spot.

She had not forgotten that vow, and neither, she was sure, had he.

Chapter Seven

The number of family members that assembled each week for the ritual of Eleanor's Thursday night dinners had increased. Both Victoria and Lorne Junior were married: she to the county school superintendent and, as anticipated, he to the daughter of a local insurance man. Both in-laws, fortunately for them, had arrived too late to the Kingston ranks to suffer unduly from Annie Jo's cooking. During a year in New York when she had tried to break into modeling, Victoria had taken a class in the culinary arts and come home to share with Annie Jo the skills she had learned. Now, besides the improvement in the food, another bright spot had been added to the Kingston table—the presence of the only Kingston grandchild, Victoria's engaging ten-year-old son, Peter.

"Aunt Aly, Aunt Aly!" the child cried in pleasure as she entered the front door of the house. Aly knew that he had been watching for her from the windows of the living room where the family was gathered for their predinner cocktails. His joy at seeing her momentarily swept aside the gloom of her thoughts.

"Hi, mutt!" She laughed as he threw his arms around her waist. He was a handsome little boy, having inherited a striking combination of physical features from his parents—Victoria's blond hair and classically shaped face as well as his father's brown eyes and fine, straight teeth. "Coming out to Aly's house tomorrow afternoon?"

"You bet!" he piped. "An' I'm bringin' Chuck 'n' Andrew 'n' Timmy—"

"And no more," remonstrated his mother, coming out into the hall. "Three of your friends are enough to spend the night at Aunt Aly's." She smiled at Aly, her cheeks as plump and shining as small apples. "He'd bring the entire fifth grade if you'd let him."

"Why not?" Aly embraced her sister fondly. "There's plenty of room, and they do have the best time."

"Well, you'll have to let me supply the food. I have a new cake recipe I want to try anyway."

Taking her nephew's hand, Aly swung it between them as they entered the living room, suggesting a mood she did not feel. "Hello, everybody," she greeted her family, deciding to get it over with. "Guess who's in town?"

Victoria seemed to have taken the news as uncomfortably as their father, Aly was thinking, looking over her coffee cup at the subdued expression of her sister. The earlier lighthearted mood so characteristic of her had vanished, leaving the merry fullness of her face lax with dour introspection.

Aly wondered sympathetically if Marshall's return made Victoria regret all the weight she had gained when she was pregnant with Peter. And not only that, Aly observed reluctantly, there had also been a general decline in Victoria's looks over the last ten years. Noting the haphazard hairdo and unbecoming dress, Aly concluded this was more because of inattention to grooming than a real loss of beauty. Neither husband nor son seemed to mind. Victoria was an integral part of their athletic and outdoor pursuits—interests that were not conducive to rigid diets and beauty routines.

Until just now, Victoria had not seemed to mind either. "I gave up Dr. Stillman for James Beard!" was her usual laughing response to startled friends who had not seen her for a long time. After her marriage, a new Victoria had emerged—happy, comfortable with herself, and a marked improvement on the sister Aly used to know. The two of them had become the best of friends.

It had been a surprise to them all that Victoria had married Warren Sims, a fourth-grade teacher with whom she had taught in Oklahoma City. Ordinary in appearance except for his quiet smile and warm brown eyes, he was the kind of man not likely to leave an impression at a first meeting. But Warren was discovered to be the type in whom still waters run deep. Time and association revealed a wit and humor, a wisdom and an intelligence that made him a favorite of them all.

At first the family had feared the worst when Victoria brought him home on her return from New York and announced that they were a month married. Eleanor's incisive eye had shot at once to her daughter's waistline, and she had consulted her husband about the wisdom of finding Warren a teaching position somewhere out of state, perhaps Alaska. But Peter was not born until a full eight months later, an event that proved disappointing to the local keepers-of-the-calendar for such occasions. Lorne Senior had then manipulated circumstances that brought his grandson and daughter home permanently from Oklahoma City. He simply arranged to have his new son-in-law instated as principal in one of the local elementary schools.

Now, glancing up to catch Aly's eye, Victoria smiled absently, but Aly had seen her sister's sad expression. Nostalgia had glazed over the still-beautiful blue eyes, and Aly suspected that Victoria had gone back into the past for a visit with the girl she once had been.

"Aly, may I see you in the study?" Lorne Senior asked as the family gathered in the hall making their farewells.

"Of course," she said, guessing that his long face had to do with Marshall.

"Have you had an offer over the last few years to buy your bank stock?" Lorne asked immediately after the door was shut.

"Kingston State Bank stock? Are you kidding? Right now I doubt if I could give it away."

"Don't be impertinent," Lorne said sharply, tugging at the collar of his white shirt. Not since Elizabeth had cared for them had he had a shirt whose collar did not chafe.

"What's the reason for the question, Dad? You look more worried than usual tonight. I thought the bank was starting a slow turnaround."

"Oh, it is, it is," Lorne dismissed her remark irritably.

"Then what's the matter? Why did you ask about my stock?"

"I found out this week that several members of the board have been approached over the last few years by an out-of-state firm wanting to buy their shares. Recently they were approached again."

"Were they offered a good price?"

"Yes, that's what puzzles me. Why would anyone want to buy bank stock considerably above its book value?"

"Maybe the stock is expected to go up?" At Lorne's chastising look, she said, "Well, so what if a tender offer is made for the outstanding shares? We're still the majority stockholder." From the way her father took a seat at his desk, Aly felt compelled to ask, "Aren't we?"

Lorne shook his gray head. "Not anymore. I...had to sell a

substantial number of my shares to cover some personal loans. The family is no longer in possession of the majority of the stock."

Aly approached the desk incredulously. "You mean that— that you're no longer in control of the bank?"

"That is *not* what I mean!" Lorne trounced vehemently on such a heresy. "The board members own nine percent among them. They're loyal to me. They would never sell. And with each of you children owning ten percent and with my ten..."

"That totals forty-nine percent," Aly said, her glance steady, "still not a majority."

"It's a damn good furlong ahead of anybody else," her father declared.

"Who has the rest of the shares?"

"Dear Lord, Aly!" Over the top of his glasses, Lorne leveled a reproving look. "Don't you ever read the annual report?"

"Nonfiction is more my line," Aly said flatly, inferring that the impressive publication of the bank's assets and liabilities yearly sent to the shareholders glossed over the facts. It also listed the names of those owning stock in the bank.

Lorne ignored the implication. "Hattie Handlin owns ten percent. The rest is divided among four out-of-state firms who have purchased them at irregular intervals through the years."

"So we're talking about an outstanding fifty-one percent."

"Yes, and I'm not worried that those big eastern stockholders will join ranks with Hattie and try to wrest control of the bank from me. Their proxies have always been favorably disposed toward the board's recommendations..."

"The major one being your renomination as president and chairman," Aly said slowly, more to herself than to her father.

"Exactly," Lorne returned with satisfaction. "It just makes

me uncomfortable to know that I'm not leaving Lorne Junior sitting in as secure a position as I enjoyed."

"Are you worried that Marshall might be behind the purchase of those out-of-state shares?" Aly asked, watching her father's expression carefully. "Suppose Hattie is approached about her shares? Suppose she sells? That would give somebody out there," she waved an arm, "fifty-one percent of stock."

"I'm perfectly capable of making my own calculations, Aly," Lorne snapped, confirming to his daughter that she had struck a nerve. "If I could just find out how much the stock was sold for, the details of the transactions, but none of the original shareholders will tell me anything."

"Is that so surprising? You dumped your stock when you saw the sky about to fall, sold it high to people who had been your friends for years..."

"That's just a guess on your part, Aly."

"I know you, Dad, so I don't have to guess. Why don't you buy Hattie's stock, if you're so worried. Then you'd at least have control of fifty percent."

"I tried to," Lorne admitted, "but she wouldn't sell to me."

"Oh, Dad, how you have made friends and influenced your enemies," said Aly dryly. "So what do you think? Is Marshall involved with this? It's strange that he's in town less than two weeks before the annual stockholders' meeting to re-elect the board. Have those out-of-state firms sent in their proxies?"

"No," Lorne answered, looking away with a thoughtful frown. "They're usually in by now. Hattie hasn't voted, either, but she's usually at the meeting to cast her vote against the board in person. However, I have no reason to believe the proxies won't be favorable. I'll just rest easier when they're in." He brought his glance back to focus confidently on Aly. "No, to answer your question about Marshall, I don't think he has anything to do with this. I can't imagine why he's back in town. Probably he's come back to gloat, now that he's made it and we've fallen on bad times. That would be typical of a dirt-farmer's son."

Aly viewed her father gravely. "For your sake as well as Lorne Junior's, I hope you're right," she said, and left the room.

The next morning, Aly woke early and took her coffee out onto the back porch, from which she could view the precise, manicured layout of Green Meadows Breeding Farm. In the first light of dawn, the green, white-fenced acres sparkled with dewy perfection and serenity.

Aly always began her day from here. In the five years she had lived in her house, the early morning scene had never failed to rouse in her an appreciation of her good fortune, to fill her with the joy of possession. From here, perspectives were gained, proportions took shape, fears quieted. From here, sipping her coffee, she was able to slay the dragons that attacked in the night.

This morning, though, the demons would not be stilled. The anxious questions that had tormented her sleep still trailed behind her, demanding and persistent. Why had Marshall returned to Claiborne? Did his presence here have anything to do with the stockholders' meeting in two weeks? What would be his reaction to her house should he happen to see it? How would he feel about what had happened to Cedar Hill? And how did she feel about Marshall? Did he have the power to hurt her again? When he had gone, would she be left as bruised, as empty, as lost as he had left her before?

Aly looked out across the early spring peace of her fields and paddocks. Today the scene did not soothe and edify. This morning she felt tired and sore and tender. She felt eighteen again.

The telephone rang, its sudden, unexpected interruption causing her to spill her coffee. Good Lord, but she was jumpy! The caller was her stable manager. His aunt had taken ill early this morning, he explained, and he'd had to call an ambulance to take her to the hospital. He would not be out to Green Meadows until she was stabilized.

"Take as long as you need, Joe," Aly told him in concern. "Willy and I can manage."

She glanced at the clock as she hung up. She would have to hurry now if she was to give herself the extra attention she had planned before she left for the office. Joe usually opened up for her and was to have been on hand this morning for the delivery of two mares to be serviced by Green Meadows studs.

Marshall drove through the wrought-iron gates of Claiborne's one cemetery and followed the road around to two pink marble monuments identical in size and shape. He parked his car and got out, standing a moment by the white Lincoln before walking slowly toward the twin memorials he had ordered to mark the graves of his parents. The muscle of his heart contracted as he reached them and stood looking down at the names etched in stone.

His father had not lived long when the sale of Cedar Hill to a residential development company had forced him and his mother off the land. The company intended to begin construction at once, as Lorne Kingston had known when he told Sy Wayne that he could stay at Cedar Hill until a buyer could be found. The buyer had been in the wings even before the foreclosure. The farm had been resold immediately for an incorporated city designed to house the growing number of highly paid oil executives working in Oklahoma City. Unfortunately for Sy Wayne, but as previously agreed, the buyer had taken it off the bank's hands for the exact sum that had been invested in it, so the Waynes did not realize a profit. Lorne Kingston, however, as a silent partner in the development company, realized plenty. The discovery had driven another nail into the Kingston coffin.

His parents had not been able to find a place to live in Claiborne and had gone to Texas, where they went to work as caretakers of a small farm in the eastern part of the state. To Marshall's sorrow and exasperation, they had refused to accept any help from their son, arguing that he needed every cent he made to live in New York and that they had the ten thousand that Aly had paid for Sampson.

It wasn't quite two months later that Elizabeth went to the back door of the shabby little farmhouse and called down to her husband in the barn that supper was ready. In that hour before nightfall, he had gone to mend a couple of harnesses from the Cedar Hill days. Elizabeth called again, but Sy did not come. She said later that she had known what she would find, and she had turned off all the burners before she ran down to the barn. She found Sy lying face-up in the straw, the harnesses still clutched in his hand. Death had caught his countenance in the anguish that Marshall knew had stilled his heart.

He had persuaded his mother to come live with him in New York. Marshall bought her the first fine clothes she had ever owned and a mink jacket her second Christmas in the city. But her eyes mirrored always the memories of another place, another life, and she began to fade. When the realization hit Marshall that something besides homesickness and grief was wrong with his mother, it was too late.

"Mother, there is radiation. There's cobalt and drugs. God, there are lots of things that can be done!"

"No, son."

"Mother, *please*—"

"No, Marshall."

He had brought her body home to be buried beside his father in the company of friends they had loved. From time to time he wondered about the graves on the windswept hill, if they were being cared for properly. Now he saw that they were. Somebody had planted flowers before the headstones, red geraniums like the kind his mother had grown in clay pots on the steps at Cedar Hill.

The unexpected kindness moved him, and blinking hard, he bent down and yanked at a grass runner attempting to encroach on the territory of one of the plants. He had expected pain in coming back. Claiborne was a reminder of all his losses. All that he had ever loved or cared about had been here, and now there was nothing to come home to. But he would change that. He would belong in Claiborne again. He had come to take back what was his.

He stood up, brushing dirt from his hands, gazing at the stones. *Mom...Dad...I've come home. Nothing will ever make your son leave again.* The thought was comforting as he walked away toward his car.

Five minutes later, Marshall pulled off the road alongside the white split-rail fence that marked the boundary of Cedar Hill. *Now that's a nice change from the barbed wire of the old days,* he thought, his eye following the well-groomed line of railings down the highway to where he knew it must merge with those of Green Meadows Breeding Farm. He had learned a few years ago that Matt Taylor had purchased Cedar Hill when the development company had failed, a natural enough move since Green Meadows butted against one side and the back of its property line. Marshall had been relieved at the time. At least the land would not be sold in parcels, making it more difficult to buy it back. Now he only hoped he could strike a bargain with the tight-fisted old piker. Matt should be close to retirement now and glad of a chance to sell off some of his holdings. Marshall planned to offer him a price his Yankee principles of economics would not let him turn down.

Marshall's approving gaze swept over the immaculate rolling acres where healthy horses grazed in the early spring sunshine. A wide, well-paved road ran up to the hill that had given the farm its name. Matt had replanted the cedars, Marshall was glad to see, and it was his guess that they screened a compound of barns built on the same spot as his former home. He'd have to do something about that in time.

The scene was quite a contrast from the last time he had stood here. He had come to bury his mother. The gate had been padlocked then, and he'd been glad that she had been spared the sight of what was once her home. The house and pecan trees, the cedars, the fields and barns had all been destroyed, of course. In their place had been left an abandoned construction site of what was to have been a posh city for the oil executives pouring into Okalahoma City in those days. Marshall had surveyed the unfinished roads, cracked slabs, and half-constructed buildings, their structures like unsightly skeletons in the raw dusk of that winter's day, until hatred for the man responsible had blinded his vision. Not even knowing that Kingston had lost millions on the failed project comforted him. What a sweet deal the man thought he'd had!

Lorne had not banked on a partner in the land company as unscrupulous as he. By the time the first foundations were poured on Cedar Hill, charges had been brought against the company for land fraud in another part of the country. Kingston awoke one morning to read in the paper that his partner, rather than face allegations, had absconded with what was left of the firm's assets. Bankruptcy proceedings immediately followed, tying up the land in litigation for a number of years, and finally Matt Taylor had bought Cedar Hill.

Shaking off his memories, Marshall turned away and made for his car. He was eager to get on with the next phase in his plans.

Aly looked up from her desk in Matt Taylor's former office and through the wide windows saw the white Continental turn into the entrance of Green Meadows. She had been expecting it. All morning she had looked up every few minutes, hoping, dreading to see the car coming down the drive, growing more anxious with each hour that passed. For years she had conditioned herself for this moment. She had always known that one day Marshall would return to Claiborne, and she had planned what she would say and do when they met face-to-face. It had been a goal in her life, their meeting. She had hoped fate would allow her to be ready for him. She deserved that. This morning as she had chosen her clothes and spent longer than usual on her makeup and hair, she had been grateful for the forewarning she'd received. Marshall wouldn't catch her by surprise. She would meet him looking her best, her speech rehearsed, her manner prepared.

Now, seeing him get out of the car and walk by the windows to the door, all her fortifications blew away like leaves in the wind. She felt a sense of betrayal, a helpless outrage at herself that she should sit here like this, going pale, blank, and numb—when she had functioned so admirably in her dreams.

Marshall had his head down, concerned with the mat that looked as if it might catch under the door when he opened it, and did not see her immediately. When he did, a tremor of surprised pleasure passed through him. "I knew you looked familiar," he said with a smile and approached the desk. She had hazel eyes, very clear and bright. Their expression distressed him slightly. It reminded him of the startled look of a fawn, wary of the sudden appearance of the hunter. For one so pretty, she was amazingly shy. He asked very kindly, "Who are you?"

She was really quite regal when she stood, Marshall thought. He wondered if habit or nerves caused her to balance with her fingertips pressed to the desk, like an executive addressing a board meeting. He felt as if he'd been shot in the chest when she said, "Aly Kingston, Marshall. Welcome home."

His smile vanished immediately. It couldn't be. Not this svelte, golden-haired beauty. To steady himself, he reached inside of his casual outdoor jacket and brought out a cigarette. "What happened to you?" he asked, a mild frost cooling his tone.

"What do you mean?"

"You know what I mean. You," he indicated to her with the cigarette before putting it between his lips. "Aly Kingston, the stick-figure kid."

"Oh, I suppose I grew up."

"I suppose you did," he mocked, snapping the lighter shut and taking a chair. Aly sat down also. He swept a look over her. "You used to have hair that hung in your eyes and looked like dried straw. Now it's...different," he amended his original thought.

"I finally bowed to the wonder-working miracle of a permanent."

"You should have bowed sooner. What happened to your freckles? There were hundreds of them as I remember."

"They faded."

"And your teeth? Weren't they sort of bucked?"

"Braces, when I was a freshman in college."

"In college?" The dark brows arched. "I seem to recall that college was not in your plans."

"Well, my plans were changed for me. I got a degree in animal science after I'd become interested in horses when I worked for Matt."

"Where is Matt anyway? He's the man I've come to see."

Aly hesitated only long enough to push an ashtray toward him. "Matt had a coronary about six years ago and had to retire. He lives in Florida now."

Marshall sat up straighter. The rich brown eyes were very still. From their depths flashed the hard glitter of deeply buried topazes. "Did he sell Green Meadows?"

"Yes," she answered.

"Who bought the place?"

"Me."

Shock vibrated through him. He sat paralyzed for the time it took him to assimilate this new information. Aly Kingston owned Green Meadows? Then that meant that she...Good God! Why had he never considered that possibility?

"Yes, Marshall," she said, sympathetically reading his deduction, "I own what used to be Cedar Hill. As you are obviously aware, Matt bought it after the development company went broke."

Marshall's mouth twisted. "No wonder you didn't acknowledge me in the airport."

Aly flushed, beginning to get a little angry. "Well, there were other reasons, too. We didn't part the best of friends, you may recall. You say you came to see Matt. Would your visit have anything to do with Sampson?"

Marshall took a deep drag on the cigarette. Smoke wafted out of his nose before he answered. "He's the reason I'm here, yes. Is he still at Green Meadows?" It was only half a lie. Sampson was one of two reasons he had driven out here today.

"Yes," Aly said, able to smile for the first time. "He's still here. Sampson is one of my top breeding stallions. Would you like to see him? He's having a little rest from his chores today."

"Sounds like some job that boy has gotten himself. Yes, I'd like to see him."

Aly consulted a chart on the wall. "He's in the west paddock. I'll have to take you out there myself. My stable manager is out today, and I can't spare one of the men to go with you. We can walk from here." She reached for a blazer with the insignia of Green Meadows on the pocket. Marshall stubbed out his cigarette and stood up as she came from around the desk. His jacket, plaid shirt, and jeans appeared new, Aly noticed. In contrast, his boots were old and scuffed, beyond the claim of shoe polish. She recognized them from the Cedar Hill days. Had he kept the boots for sentiment, or did they represent some kind of symbol to him, like the white Continental?

"Sampson can't be the only reason you've returned to Claiborne," Aly commented as they walked down the bridle path.

"He isn't. I'm treating myself to a little vacation. I haven't had one in a long time."

"You've come to Claiborne for a vacation?" Her tone was patently skeptical.

"What better place for some peace and quiet?"

She refused to glance his way. "You bring your family with you?"

He gave a mirthless laugh, perceiving her motive in asking. "You should know the answer to that. You were with me on the flight. I'm not married. I haven't had time for a wife and children. The family I had is buried at the edge of town. What about you?"

Aly shook her head. "I've been busy, too," she said, her heart twisting at his last remark. "Marshall—about Elizabeth and Sy—you know how sorry I am."

"Yes," he said, "I know." They had reached their destination. Marshall looked out upon the empty paddock. "I don't see him," he said.

"He's there," Aly assured him. "Over behind that feeding shed. Marshall," she warned, "he may not remember you."

"He'll remember me," he said with certainty. "Just see if he doesn't."

They stood in silence for a few moments, Marshall waiting for the stallion to sense his presence as he had done in years past when he returned from college. Aly stole a look at him. His nearly black hair was still sumptuously full and untouched by gray, even at the temples. His complexion had the high color of good health and his body the lean look of a man who kept himself physically fit. She wondered if he ever missed the hard work, the fields and animals, the space and air of country living. Did he, she wondered, ever long to hear the sound of cowbells in the dusk?

Her attention went back to the field, and a small exclamation escaped her as Sampson ambled from behind the shed, ears pointed in their direction. Marshall's expression cleared. Years fell away. He might have been in college again, home for the summer. "Sampson!" he breathed in delight. "Just look at you, boy!"

The stallion was certainly a grand sight, Aly allowed, feeling a thrill of pride. The late morning sun gleamed on the high shine of his reddish brown coat and the smooth conformation of powerfully developed muscles. He did not move but watched warily as Marshall opened the gate.

Sampson, remember him, Aly urged silently as Marshall

walked across the paddock toward the motionless horse, harness in hand. At the sound of his name called by the stranger coming toward him, the stallion whinnied softly and twitched his tail, his attitude guarded and vigilant. *He won't come if he doesn't recognize him*, she thought, saying a prayer that Sampson would not break and run as Marshall neared. That was a favorite devilment of his when her horsemen tried to catch him at night, and one that she'd never taken many pains to break him from. Sampson stood still only for Willy or Joe to slip a harness over his head.

Now her heart held as Marshall stopped. He dropped the harness, clapped his hands, and gave a short, clear whistle. "Sampson," he called, and Aly could hear the emotion in his voice, "don't you remember me, boy? It's Marshall. It's Marshall come home."

Unable to breathe, Aly watched as the animal cautiously moved forward, sniffing the air. Marshall stayed where he was, and when the stallion drew nearer, put out his hand as he had done when the horse had come to greet him all those school vacations ago. Suddenly Sampson's head arched, his tail hiked. He gave a loud neigh and began to trot the rest of the way toward Marshall. Aly's vision blurred as the two met in the paddock in a joyous reunion. Thirteen years. Sampson remembered after thirteen years. *Some of us never forget, do we, boy?*

Marshall smiled and waved at her as he slipped the harness over Sampson's head. At the gate Aly waved back, watching as Marshall mounted to canter bareback around the paddock, man and horse a magnificent pair. How much at home he looked up there on Sampson, she thought, with his straight back silhouetted against the Oklahoma sky—so much more like the Marshall she remembered than the man in the pinstriped suit.

"He's yours if you still want him," Aly told him when he had dismounted. "If I'd known how to get in touch with you when I bought Green Meadows, I'd have called you about him. The price is the same as our original agreement. Ten thousand dollars."

Marshall, patting the horse's neck, still absorbed in the joy of the reunion, said to her in surprise, "Why, that's awfully generous of you, Aly. I know how valuable he is to you, but I sure would like to have him back. I don't have a place to keep him now, but I will in about a month. Will your offer keep until then?"

"My offer will keep until you refuse it, Marshall."

The three of them together like this reminded Aly of another time when for a short, achingly tender few moments she and Marshall had been friends. It was a memory that had never left her, one she thought about almost always when she looked at Sampson. She would miss the stallion, her last link with Marshall. But a deal was a deal. She said with a small smile, "I think I've always kept him for you."

Marshall did not speak for a second or two. Then surprising her he touched with wonder the sweep of a blond wave that had evolved from her straight bangs. "Tell me something," he said. "Those braces. Weren't they a little rough on the school quarterback?"

She answered with a broken laugh, "The school quarterback wasn't interested in me then. I still had a long way to go."

Marshall stepped back to view her figure. "Well, you got there," he said, bringing his gaze back to her face. "Or are these curves due to some miraculous and expensive assistance also?"

"They came of their own accord about the time the braces were off." To divert the turn of the conversation, Aly said, "There's someone else here that I know you'll want to see."

"Who?"

"Willy."

Marshall stared at her in speechless astonishment before letting out a whoop of pleasure. "Willy, here? Where in the world did you find him, Aly? I thought he'd disappeared for good when Dad died."

"I did, too. I had to hire a detective agency to track him down. When I got in touch with him I offered him a job."

"How did you get him working around horses again? Give him one of those offers that can't be refused?"

So he remembered, she thought, and without rancor, too. He was grinning. Aly said with a smile, "You might say that. I offered him a home."

Marshall smiled his approval. "So the old fellow has a home again."

"For as long as he lives, if he wants it. He's up at the main barn this morning. I'll let you surprise him. He'll be so happy to see you. Well," Aly took a breath and extended her hand, "good-bye, Marshall. It was good to see you again. Call when you want to pick up Sampson. I'll have the sale agreement ready. My stable manager, Joe Handlin, will take care of you. Have a good vacation."

Marshall said slowly, "Why not you? Why won't you be taking care of me?" His hand closed around hers reluctantly.

"Oh," she shrugged, "this time of year when the breeding season is well under control, I usually take buying trips. I doubt that I'll be here when you come again." She drew her hand away, gave him a brief smile, a curt nod. "So long," she said formally and left him to walk back toward her office, glad that he could not see the tears that filled her eyes.

Back at her desk, she blinked them away quickly and turned over in her mind the questions Marshall had not asked, wondering if their omission was by design or from lack of interest.

He hadn't inquired about her family, her marital status, or where she lived. He had made no comment about Cedar Hill.

She did not believe for a second that he was here for a vacation. She might accept that he had returned to buy Sampson from Matt Taylor, but why appear just at this time? He could have well afforded the horse before now. And this place he said would be available in a month. Where was it? How long did he plan to stay in Claiborne on this...vacation?

A blue station wagon turning into the entrance of Green Meadows gave her a shock. Good heavens, it was Victoria, and in the back were four small bobbing heads. Aly glanced at the clock. She had forgotten that they would be out this early since school had been dismissed at noon today for a statewide teachers meeting.

The Continental was still parked in front. Aly pushed back her chair, hoping she could get rid of her sister before Marshall returned to his car. She knew how Victoria looked during the day and wanted to spare her the embarrassment of meeting an old heartthrob in a faded housedress and slippers. But just as she got up, Marshall rounded the corner. In no hurry, he waited for the blue station wagon to pull in alongside the Continental. *Oh, damn!* Aly muttered in consternation, seeing Victoria's stark, gaping look as she spotted him. She only hoped that Marshall, used to that kind of feminine reaction, would not recognize her, but at his double take, she hurried out.

"Victoria?" Marshall was asking. "Victoria Kingston?" He seemed planted to the spot.

"Victoria Sims now," Aly informed him breezily, stepping between him and the station wagon to block Marshall's view. She waved to the happy, noisy little boys bouncing around in the backseat. "Hello, guys!" she sang out, hoping the diversionary tactic would give Victoria a few seconds to compose herself.

Victoria rolled down the window, her pale lips twitching uncertainly. "Is that Marshall?" she asked.

"Yes," Aly answered with a strained smile, conscious that Marshall was coming around to join them.

Victoria looked up at the handsome face appearing over Aly's shoulder, smiling faintly. "Just a minute and I'll get out," she said in a small voice. Aly could have sunk through the ground for her. Victoria was attired in her most unbecoming tent dress. "I'm not dressed for meeting old friends," she apologized, tucking a loose strand of fair hair back into a careless topknot.

"Certainly you are," said Marshall, and Aly blessed him for his warmth. He held out his hand. "How are you, Victoria?"

"As you can see," she laughed nervously, "a little heavier, but very happy, Marshall. What brings you back to Claiborne?"

"I'm on vacation."

"Vacation? In Claiborne? With your kind of money?"

"Well, you know what they say," Marshall responded easily. "There's no accounting for taste."

"No, I guess not," Victoria said uncomfortably. She addressed her sister. "I just came by to get the key to the house. Don't worry about lunch. I packed each of the boys a sack to take with them when they go exploring, and I bought you and me chicken salad with French bread and wine..." Her voice trailed off in embarrassment.

Marshall took the hint. "Well, ladies, I won't keep you. Nice to see you again, Victoria. Aly, Willy looks great. I'm grateful to you." He waved at the two women and started for his car.

"Marshall, don't go just yet," Aly called to him. "Victoria, go on up to the house. I'll be along in a minute. I think the boys are about to explode to get out. There's lemonade in the fridge." She handed her sister a key.

Watching the station wagon drive off, Aly asked quietly of Marshall, "Surprised?"

"Very. I hope it didn't show."

"Not at all. Now it's my turn to be grateful."

"She was so beautiful once. She's married, I take it."

"Yes. Her little boy Peter was in the backseat. He was the one with the very blond hair and dark eyes. A wonderful little guy."

"What happened that she...changed so."

Slightly irritated, Aly said, "Being a man, you may not be able to discern this about Victoria, Marshall, but happiness is what happened to her. Right after coming back from New York, she married a great guy who loves her for something other than her looks."

"Hey," Marshall soothed. "You don't have to defend Victoria against me. More power to her if she's happy."

"I thought all Kingstons had to be defended against you."

He examined her face as he thought about how best to answer that charge. Aly Kingston was actually as much of a shock to him as her sister had been.

"Victoria is not on the list," he said.

"But the rest of us are, is that it?" Aly demanded. A strand of golden hair had blown across her lips, and Marshall noticed how sensitively shaped they were.

"You're fast getting off it. It's hard to hold a grudge against a lady who has been as good to my two old friends as you've been. Besides, you're awfully pretty. See you, Aly."

As he drove off, Aly hoped he had meant that last remark.

She found Victoria in the kitchen removing things from a picnic basket. She suspected that her sister had begun humming when she heard Aly coming in the front door. "Marshall looked good," Victoria said casually.

"Yes, didn't he?" agreed Aly, taking down two wineglasses.

She preferred not to drink at midday since alcohol made her sleepy. Victoria, she knew, would go home and take a nap. "May I ask you something?" she asked.

"Ask away," said Victoria.

"Did you know Marshall in New York?"

Victoria turned to her in the gesture disclaiming surprise she had perfected as a youngster. Aly could see through it clearer than water. "Know Marshall in New York? Why, of course not. Whatever made you ask such a thing? Don't you think I would have mentioned it?"

"Then why did you say 'with *your* kind of money' a while ago?"

"Oh, I don't know," Victoria replied, licking at the icing that had spread and cooled around the edge of the cake board. "I suppose because of the Lincoln Continental."

"It could have been rented."

"Oh for goodness' sake, Aly, how would I know?"

Aly knew Victoria was lying. Wetting her lips nervously, she said, "Victoria, forgive me. I wouldn't upset you for the world and I don't want to pry. But this is important. Marshall is back in Claiborne for a reason, and I don't think it has anything to do with a vacation. Marshall could have easily known you were in New York twelve years ago. I wrote Elizabeth when she lived with Marshall that you had gone. I even told her the name of the modeling agency you were working for. Did Marshall get in touch with you? Did he get you to fall in love with him, then drop you as punishment for being a Kingston? Is that why you married Warren so suddenly when you got back—on the rebound?"

Victoria, her blue eyes wide with astonishment, gaped at her sister. "Alyson, have you gone insane? What an absurd notion! Don't you dare go dragging out your speculations around Mother and Dad, do you hear me? What has gotten into you?"

Aly went to her sister and touched her face gently. "Victoria, Marshall Wayne threatened to get even with Dad, you know, one way or the other. What better way than through his children? If he's back to seek vengeance against the rest of us, I think we have a right to know."

"Well, little sister," Victoria said icily, throwing things back into the basket, "if I had known your precious Marshall in New York, wouldn't Elizabeth have known? She was alive at the time. Did she ever mention me to you in her letters? No, I can see she didn't," Victoria said hotly, glancing at Aly's expression. "How could you accuse me of—of marrying Warren on the rebound! The very idea!" She grasped the picnic basket. "You, my dear, have just talked yourself out of a delightful chicken salad lunch. Tell the boys I'll pick them up tomorrow afternoon." She slammed the back door.

"Aunt Aly, who was the man at Green Meadows today?"

"A man who grew up in Claiborne. He's your mother's age. He lives in New York now."

"Did you like him?"

"I liked him."

"Did he like you?"

"No."

"Then how come you liked him?"

"It wasn't for the way he treated me, but for the way he treated others that I liked him. Marshall was always very kind and thoughtful to everyone else, especially his parents. He never hurt anyone that I know of."

"Then how come Mother is afraid of him?"

"Is she, you think?"

"Her hands were shaking when we left, and she didn't introduce me like she always does."

"Well, darling, your mother was startled at seeing Marshall. She wasn't dressed to meet him, you see. We women like to look our best when handsome men from the past come back to visit. You'll see someday when you're every bit as handsome as Marshall. You'll make many a girl shiver and quake."

"But he has dark hair and I have blond."

"Well, blond men are handsome, too. Especially, tall, dark-eyed blond men. Now go to sleep, sweetheart. Your compadres are already long into dreamland."

Later, out on the porch, Aly reflected on the conversation she'd had with her nephew. Was what Peter had noticed in his mother actually fear, panic, or piqued vanity? Aly was almost certain that Victoria and Marshall had gotten together in New York—maybe even had an affair. The knowledge hurt and saddened her—angered her, too. It was clear who had come out on the short end of the stick. Marshall had had his little fling with the beautiful daughter of the man he despised, then cast her aside like a dirty shirt. Scratch a line through Victoria Kingston. Who was next on the list?

The phone rang. She answered it quickly so the children would not be disturbed. It was probably Joe, calling to inform her about his aunt.

But it was Marshall. "Aly? Marshall Wayne. I hope I'm not calling too late."

"No," she said, her heart in her throat. "I was still up. What can I do for you?"

"I had dinner with Willy tonight." Dinner. In the past, it had been supper.

"How nice. What has that to do with me?"

"He told me about Benjy Carter. I owe you an apology, Aly. It's thirteen years overdue. May I see you tomorrow night?"

Emotions warred within her. She wanted to see him, but she didn't. This was probably how he had entrapped Victoria. "Well, I—did Willy tell you where I live?"

"No, but I'm sure I can find it." The tone was somewhat dry. "I'll take you somewhere for dinner. Jimmy's still open?"

"Yes. It's bigger and better than ever."

"Then let's go there. Seven o'clock be all right with you?"

"Yes," said Aly, her mouth dry. "I'll be ready."

"So where do I pick you up?"

"At my house, Marshall, here on Cedar Hill."

Chapter Eight

The next evening as she dressed for her dinner date, Aly felt almost nauseated from anticipation. All day she had been immersed in her thoughts of Marshall, so deeply submerged, in fact, that Joe Handlin had been compelled at one point to snap his fingers before her eyes and holler, "Hello in there! Anybody home?"

She had shot up from the depths of her contemplation so fast that she had weaved uncertainly, unable to focus clearly on Joe's concerned face. "Aly? You okay?"

"Yes, Joe. Just preoccupied, that's all."

"Wouldn't have anything to do with Marshall Wayne, would it?"

"Now, Joe, don't be jealous."

"Why shouldn't I be? I don't need Marshall coming in here warming himself at a fire that I've been trying to kindle."

"You're crude sometimes, Joe. Did you know that?"

"I love you, Aly."

"I know."

Joe Handlin, like Sampson, had come with the purchase of Green Meadows. Before then, the facts about the night Lady Loverly aborted her foal had come to light, thanks to Benjy Carter's "getting religion" after he realized the horrible truth of what alcohol addiction had forced him to do. Benjy, tearful, repentant, and fearing for his soul, had gone to Matt and confessed that he had been promised by "a man over the telephone," payment of his bail and enough liquor to see him through Christmas if he would do what had to be done to get Aly Kingston fired. He hadn't wanted to do it, but the hounds of hell were eating him alive, and he'd have killed his own mother for one drink. Learning the truth, Joe had felt so guilty over the matter that on his day off he had driven to Norman where Aly was attending college to apologize in person for wrongfully accusing her. She had been grateful for his invaluable assistance when she took over Green Meadows, but with it had come an affection that she neither encouraged nor wanted. His feelings could make for a tricky situation if she saw much of Marshall, a possibility that might be likely now that she, too, had been removed from his list.

At four o'clock when she finished making her rounds of the stables, Willy had limped with her down to her office. "I enjoyed having supper with young Marshall last night, Punkin. It's so good to see him again. I'd often wondered about him, what had happened to him when his folks died."

"It's been my guess that he's been busy making money...and remembering."

"You got both those right, kiddo."

"You sound worried."

"I am a mite. I think a right smart of the boy, but I'd be mighty put out with him if he included you in anything he might have in mind for your pa. He ain't got no cause to hurt you, Aly, none a'tall. Cedar Hill came to you fair and square. I hope you didn't mind, but I told him how it was that you came to lose Sampson and your job with Matt Taylor."

"I don't mind. I'm glad you did. It clears the air on that score at least. What makes you think Marshall plans to hurt us?"

"It's not anything he said. It's just a feeling I had when I looked at him, heard him talk. Has he seen the house yet?"

"No. He'll see it tonight. He's taking me to Jimmy's."

When Victoria arrived shortly afterward to pick up the boys, she had shooed them into the station wagon without much more than a hello to Aly.

"Victoria, what is the matter?"

"Did you boys tell Aunt Aly that you had a good time?"

To their choruses of *yes*, Victoria had bunched the fullness of her tent dress around her thighs and slid beneath the wheel. "Nothing is the matter with me, Aly. You upset me yesterday, that's all." Without another word she had driven off, leaving Aly staring after her in deep concern.

At her dressing tables, Aly consulted herself in the mirror. *Old sins cast long shadows.* That had been a favorite maxim of her grandmother's, quoted often in the presence of her only child. Aly wished her father had taken heed. His sins stood to cast their shadows over the lot of them. Who of them would suffer the most from the menace of their shade?

Slowing his car at the gate of Cedar Hill, Marshall looked up at the spiky green sentinels guarding the hill. *So she'd built herself a house, had she?* he thought in chagrin, *and on the exact spot where his family's had been*, he'd bet. He might have guessed as much when Aly told him she'd purchased Green Meadows. Well, for the moment he'd push that problem aside and deal with it later when he'd successfully dispensed with the first one.

Unease rode high in his chest, like a hiatus hernia. Things were not going as smoothly as he'd planned. Hattie Handlin had not been answering her phone. Yesterday her nephew had not been at work. Were the two circumstances related, and did they imply trouble for him? He couldn't afford to show the smallest interest in either one. The news was out that he was in town. His bitterness over the foreclosure had not been forgotten, nor, it seemed, his promise to Kingston. A mere mention that he'd inquired about Hattie—or even Joe—would be enough for some people in certain quarters to know why he'd showed up just now. He'd just have to sit tight and wait until tomorrow.

Also his feelings for Aly worried him. He shouldn't be seeing her tonight, but he was one who always paid his debts, and he owed Aly Kingston. Last night he'd gone to bed full of shame after Willy's disclosure about Benjy Carter. So old man Kingston had been responsible for Aly losing her job, had he? God, what a reprobate! He remembered the day she had explained about Sampson, and how he'd disbelieved her and told her he never wanted to see her again. He could still see the look on her face, though he hadn't thought of it since. That had been unforgivably cruel of him. He had known of her slavish devotion to him since grade school. His mouth twisted wryly. Aly and her deals. How like her to make such an offer to Matt in the first place.

She was a fine human being. There was no other way to describe her. He appreciated now how hard for her it had been growing up in her family. His mother had described Aly Kingston as an orphan of the saddest kind, the kind abandoned within the home. Aly'd been wonderful to Willy, and she'd loved and revered his parents. Those geraniums up at the cemetery—they were Aly's doing.

Still, it bothered him to think that now he owed her consideration. He wanted nothing or no one to interfere with the sweet, pure, unadulterated joy he expected to feel when he deposed Lorne Kingston, when he plucked away his son's birthright as Kingston had done his. True, right or wrong, the man was Aly's father; the son, her brother. It would be her family's livelihood that he would be taking away, and for all their differences, Aly loved her father.

But, he thought regretfully, that would just have to be Aly's problem. He had no intention of allowing any consideration to deflect him from the one thing that provided meaning in his life. Following the thought, Aly's house came into view.

For an astounding moment Marshall thought that, here on this soil that had borne and bred him, something had snapped in his mind. By some cerebral quirk, he was transported back into time, far, far back—back before New York and Wharton and the foreclosure, back to the days of his boyhood, back to the house on Cedar Hill. His parents had finally managed a new coat of paint. The house gleamed a crisp yellow in the last rays of the sunset. White shutters and trim stood out fresh and bright. The roof had been repaired and the oval pane of glass in the front door replaced with a clear new one.

Marshall slowed the car, peering through the windshield to impress upon his mind as many details as he could before they dimmed. But as he drove closer, he knew he was viewing no mirage, experiencing no hallucination. His heartbeat filled his ears as he realized that Aly's house was the exact replica of his boyhood home. There was the wide front porch, the swing, the broad-armed chairs with a table in between, the pots of red geraniums lining the steps. There were the two pecan trees, not as full as the ones he remembered, nor as old—nothing was as old here, but the feel of the place was the same. He stared beyond the pecan trees, almost expecting to see a field of corn crowding the cyclone fence, to hear the clink of cowbells coming up the path, to find his father coming from the barn to meet him...

Profoundly shaken, Marshall drew to a stop before the porch steps and sat for an incredulous moment behind the wheel. Oh,

God, why had she done this? What did this mean? She could have built for herself a house of any size, style, shape, and design, but she had chosen to resurrect the house on Cedar Hill.

Throat on fire, tears hot as irons behind his eyes, he opened the car door. This was not at all what he had expected. Not at all. He had the uncomfortable, almost helpless sensation that the tables were being turned on him.

"I'm sorry," Aly said when she opened the door and saw his expression. "I should have warned you. Come in, Marshall." She stepped aside for him to enter and asked as he walked with a slight hesitation into the breezeway, "Are you...terribly shocked?"

For a moment Marshall could not answer. "It's very beautiful," he said softly.

"Come. I'll show you the rest of it."

"Let me stand here awhile first."

His first impression was that everything was as he remembered. Similar pieces of furniture—a refectory table and chairs, a hall tree, and an umbrella stand—stood against the left wall. The hall, off which familiar rooms opened, led as in former times to a back porch. The difference was that everything his eyes fell upon represented the kind of warm, gracious luxury his mother would have preferred for Cedar Hill. The back porch, for example, was not screened but jalousied to let in fresh air and light. Everywhere was air and light. He lifted his gaze to find the source of the sunset glow that filled the breezeway and discovered that a skylight served as the central section of the roof. Through it, filtered sunshine had made lush the exotic plants grouped dramatically along one wall. The other housed an aquarium in which tropical fish of breathtaking colors and iridescence swam in waters of aquamarine blue.

"Marshall?" Aly asked gently, touching his arm. When he turned to her, she saw his eyes were shadowed with memory. "Are you ready to see the rest of it?"

"Yes," he answered briefly.

"May I take your arm?"

He held it out and covered her hand with his own when she took it, as though in need of human contact. They began their journey.

It was both a trip back into the past and into a future that now would never be his. Though the rooms were larger, the colors fresher and fabrics richer than the hodgepodge with which his mother had had to make do, Aly's house was essentially unaltered from the one where he'd grown up. Some things had not changed at all. The view from the front windows was the same. The wind whistled the same tune around the corners of the chimney. In the parlor a last slant of light from the sunset struck the exact spot on the hearth where it had fallen in years past. Its extinction usually signaled the time of day his mother would come in and turn on the lamp at the end of the sofa. Releasing his arm, Aly did that now, and he started at the first light pouring out from the shade, wanting her back at his side, close to him, her hand in the crook of his arm.

She had been talking all the while on their tour, using her free hand to point out this and that while he worked through the emotion of the moment. He was grateful for her sensitivity. He could not have spoken. He was finding feelings and sensations that squeezed shut his throat and sandpapered his eyes. By the time they reached the kitchen where he had measured his growth on the pantry door, he was wondering if he could get through the evening at all.

"My old room," he managed to ask when they had circled

through to the breezeway again. "You didn't show me my old room."

"Oh," Aly said dismissively, "there's no flavor of the past there. I was only in your room once, you know."

"Is it the guest room?"

She hesitated. "No," she said after a few seconds, steering him back to the porch where she had set out ice and glasses for drinks. "It's my room."

When he was seated on the couch and watching her at the small bar built into the wall next to the kitchen—a definite innovation for Cedar Hill—Marshall decided that he couldn't face the evening without her. Even if her company wasn't what he needed, just the pleasure of looking at her would have been comforting. Tonight she was beautiful, from the golden crown of her head down to her neatly shod feet.

"Why, Aly?" he asked as she handed him a drink. "Why did you do this?"

She sat down across from him smoothing imaginary wrinkles in the lap of her denim skirt. The fiddling gave her somewhere to focus her attention, Marshall knew. Suddenly she stopped and looked directly across at him, her chin a little high. "Because," she said, "I loved the old house on Cedar Hill. I spent the happiest days of my childhood in it. Maybe because when I was there, I was the happiest with myself. In my parents' home, I was mean, spiteful, and jealous. It was only when I was at Cedar Hill that I knew a nicer me. I suppose that when the time came to have a place of my own, I just naturally thought about a house like it. I—I—know it must gall you to think of a Kingston living here in—in a house like your former home on land that you still love."

"Yes," he answered honestly, "it does somewhat. This land should still be mine, you know. I had always hoped to come back here and buy it back."

"Is that the real reason you went out to Green Meadows yesterday? Is that the reason you're back in Claiborne?"

Inwardly Marshall sighed in enormous relief. "Yes," he lied, smiling to show there were no hard feelings. "However, I concede I've been beaten to the draw."

"You're not angry, Marshall?" All at once, Aly felt much lighter, happier.

"No, I'm not angry, Aly. If Cedar Hill had to belong to anyone other than me, I'm glad it's in your hands." He took his gaze around the room appreciatively. "The house is beautiful, exactly as Mother would have liked to have seen it."

"It's a tribute to her and your father, you know, and what Cedar Hill meant to me. It's strange how this house affects everyone who spends any time in it. It's almost become the focal point of our family gatherings, oddly enough. I hope that doesn't distress you, Marshall, but you'd be gratified to see how much nicer everybody is when we gather here."

He smiled thinly. "Even your father?"

Aly nodded with a small chuckle. "Even my father. He's mellowing, Marshall."

Marshall finished his drink in a long swallow. "How about something to eat?" he asked.

Leaving the house, he walked down the porch steps behind Aly without haste. After he had seen her into the car, he paused at the door on his side and looked back at the house. He would not be able to see much of it in the darkness when he brought Aly home, and he wouldn't be back after tonight. It had been a mistake to come after all.

Jimmy's was a large, sprawling dance hall and restaurant whose outside sign declared that it served the best chicken fried steak in the state. "New Yorkers would call this paste," Marshall said, picking up a knife to cut through the white, highly peppered gravy covering the batter-coated beef. "Then they'd scrape it off and apply half a bottle of catsup."

"The height of ignorance!" responded Aly, thoroughly enjoying her first unadulterated bite of the house specialty. "Why do you stay up there among all of those uncivilized folks?"

"Because New York is the best place to do what I do best."

"Really?" Aly sounded surprised. "I can't imagine your talents limited to a geographical location."

Startled, Marshall glanced up at her, unsure of her meaning. Her expression seemed innocent enough. Under the circumstances, he should let the remark pass. But he was curious.

"And what do you think those talents may be?"

Aly could have kicked herself. The words had come out before she'd had a chance to catch hold of them. She'd hoped they'd float right by unnoticed but such was not the case. "Oh," she said casually, "I would assume the talents involved in making money."

"Is that what you would assume?"

"Yes. No—" She looked up, knowing her face must look as red as the tomato in her salad. She forced herself to meet his gaze levelly. After all, she was not eighteen anymore. She was a grown woman with every prerogative she had the nerve to take. And she'd always had plenty of nerve. "No, that is not what I meant."

Marshall thought that over in silence, their gazes holding. "I didn't think so," he said after a while and went back to his steak. He brought up the topic of Benjy Carter. "I can't apologize enough for not believing you that day," he said feelingly. "I should have known you were far too responsible to let something like that happen."

"Think no more about it, Marshall. You were in no mood

to be generous that day. Besides, everything worked out for the best. If I hadn't worked for Matt, I'd never discovered how crazy I am about horses, and if I hadn't lost Sampson, I'd never have gone to college to learn about the breeding business, and then I wouldn't have been ready to take over Green Meadows by the time I had the opportunity to buy it. Certainly it wouldn't be the success it is today."

Marshall said with a touch of rancor, "I'm sure that makes your father feel justified in what he did."

"No doubt," she said, taking a sip of wine. The specter of her father had descended between them, chilling as a sudden cloud passing over the sun. She cast about for a change of subject, but Marshall seemed determined to keep them in the past.

"When did you find out that Mother had died?"

Aly said without looking at him, because she could not be sure of her expression, "I went out to the cemetery one day to plant some geraniums by your father's headstone and found Elizabeth's grave."

"God—" He looked away from her, the blood leaving his face, appalled and sickened by his heartlessness. How could he have been so brutal to this woman whose only crime had been to love his family—and him, at one time. "Aly." He looked back at her, his eyes burning with the misery of his shame, and reached for her hand. "How can you ever forgive me? It was unconscionable of me not to let you know."

"I should have realized when my letters were returned that something terrible had happened. I should have tried to contact you in New York, but I didn't want to intrude."

"I can imagine why not," he said ruefully, still holding her hand. "I moved right after Mother died…" How could he explain to her the anguish that had led him to hurt her so? As long as he lived he would never forget the Sunday he had stood with his mother at the foot of Cedar Hill. They had been out at the cemetery to lay his father to rest. The wrecking crews had already been at the farm by then, of course. The fields had been cleared and the pens and barns demolished. The cedars lay where they had been yanked out by their roots, and the pecan trees burned to the ground. But it had been the sight of the house, gutted and crippled but still standing like some animal too proud to fall, that had broken their hearts. Nearby had stood a crane with a ramming ball suspended from its long neck, suggestive of a prehistoric beast standing guard over its helpless prey. The house had seemed to stare down at them out of its empty eyes as though aware of their shock and grief, as if it understood their helplessness to prevent what was coming in the morning. His mother had begun to sob uncontrollably, her shoulders shaking with the rending despair that would never leave her. That day the fate of the Kingstons was sealed. When his mother died two years later, he never once thought of getting in touch with a member of the family that had caused his own so much sorrow.

Aly pressed his hand in understanding, moved by his contrition and the sense of some inner grief that she could only guess at. "All apologies accepted. All forgiveness given. Let's not talk any more about the past, Marshall. Let's talk about what you've been doing with yourself these last thirteen years. And could we have more wine?" she asked, to prolong the evening. They had finished their meal and she didn't want him to take her home. Would he see her again before he returned to New York, she wondered. And how long would that be, now that Cedar Hill wasn't for sale?

Marshall released her hand to signal the waitress. While they sipped through another carafe, he told her about New York and allowed her to draw him into a discussion about investments.

"So commodities are your bag." She smiled interestedly after he'd explained the basic principles of the futures market.

Marshall patted his lips with his napkin to cover his amusement. She hadn't heard a word he'd said about trading wheat and grain futures, the financial medium through which he'd amassed a fortune. Her interest had been assumed to draw out the evening. He regretted that he wouldn't be seeing her again after tonight. "I'm out of the business now," he answered with a straight face. "Now I've opted for tax-free municipal bonds." He glanced toward the dance hall next door where a western band had struck up the first tune of the evening. Marshall folded his napkin. "Shall we go take a couple of spins around the dance floor?" he invited with a smile that only he knew was sad.

Once there, she came into his arms with the shy smile she'd always flickered when his mother said, "Say hello to Aly, son." The memory caused him to hold her protectively tighter, his arm fitting neatly around her slender waist, her hair soft against his chin. She smelled like a rain-washed morning, and he could have drowned in the freshness of her. "Hello, Aly," he whispered in her ear.

In the intimate nook of his neck and shoulder, a smile broke across her face. "Hello, Marshall," she said, remembering.

"How come you've never married?"

"I've never been asked by a man I love."

"Have there been many of those?"

"Only one."

"Anybody I know?"

"Not the way I do."

Aly felt him tense slightly, and when he did not respond, regretted the honesty of her remark. An awkward few minutes passed in which she could think of nothing to say to rescue the moment.

Apparently Marshall couldn't either. When the song ended, he smiled regretfully into her eyes. "Time I got you home," he said.

On the return trip to Cedar Hill, conversation died, leaving an uncomfortable silence. Aly thought the grief of her disappointment would burst her heart. Marshall wasn't going to see her again, she was certain. This evening had been for apologies, and now that they'd been given and forgiveness received, the chapter was closed, the missing page restored. She ought to be feeling happy now, ready to get on to other men eager to come into her life. Through the years her business had put her in touch with quite a few. She had met none whose memory could keep her awake at nights. Only one face, one smile, one man could do that. And she wondered dismally if he had not ruined her for all others.

"Will you still be wanting to buy Sampson?" she asked, the question startling in the darkness of the car.

"Why, yes," Marshall said. He cast her a look. "You say I'm to deal with Joe Handlin?"

"Yes."

"When will he be back?"

"He's back. He just took one day off."

When Aly disappointingly offered no further information, Marshall said, "I'll have to let you know later about Sampson. My plans have changed somewhat."

"Suit yourself. He'll be available."

As they drew up to the house, Aly swallowed her pride and asked, "Would you like to come in for some coffee?"

She did not look at him as she asked, and Marshall could not force himself to say no, knowing his refusal would hurt her. "Sure. That sounds good," he said, turning off the motor.

While Aly was in the kitchen preparing the coffee, Marshall stood in the summer parlor looking out at the black night. He desperately wanted a cigarette, but he would not have been comfortable smoking in this house, even though Aly had thoughtfully provided ashtrays.

It was essential that after the coffee he make a clean exit. Aly still cared for him, he thought without vanity, and he wished sincerely that she did not. Hanging around would only encourage her feelings, and she would be even more deeply hurt when he accomplished what he'd come here to do. But even without considering her, he had himself to think about. Aly Kingston was a part of him. Being with her put him in closer touch with his family, brought back all the good from the past. Being with Aly was like…going home. He could not allow those sentiments to weaken his resolve.

"Who taught you how to ride?" he asked curiously as Aly brought in a tray with two steaming coffee mugs stamped with the logo of Green Meadows.

Setting it down on the coffee table, she took a seat on the couch and asked with a wry smile, "Ever hear of the sailor who loved the sea but couldn't swim?"

Marshall looked thunderstruck. "What? Aly, you're not saying you still don't know how to ride?"

"The guy who offered to teach me blew out of town the next day."

He asked quietly, "You haven't been waiting for me to come back and teach you, have you?"

"Why not? You're here."

"Aly, listen." He longed to touch her. He wanted to sit down next to her and hold one of her cool, slender hands while he explained what he must have her understand. But he remained standing, his feet apart, looking down at her with his fingertips tucked in the pockets of his western-cut slacks. "You may be upset with me for saying this, and I won't blame you if you are, but it's got to be said."

Aly looked at him calmly, her hazel eyes lovely in the soft light. Marshall took a deep breath and hurried on. "I believe I've detected in you some feelings tonight that are carry-overs from the past. I can't imagine why you would still have them for me, given my behavior to you, but I don't think either of us can deny they're there. I—"

Though Aly remained perfectly composed, Marshall had seen the movement of a hard swallow down the sensitive line of her throat. He swore at himself and said in a plea of frustration, "Aly, what I'm trying to say is that…"

"There's someone else," Aly offered softly.

"Not someone else, Aly, *something* else, something that is a big part of my life that you could never share. Forgive me for being so blunt, for hurting you, if I have. I would never want to do that, ever again. That's why I felt it kinder to explain before I go away tonight why I won't be calling you anymore while I'm in Claiborne."

"I understand," Aly said. "I appreciate your frankness, Marshall." Damn! If she indicated by so much as an eyelash that he had just driven a two-by-four right through her, she would strangle herself before sunup. "I take it you're not going to want your cup of coffee?"

"I'm afraid not, Aly."

"Well then, let me see you to the door."

Had she, he wondered, *always had that way of rising gracefully? Where had she learned such poise if it did not come naturally?* He followed her down the breezeway, noting how the moonlight, streaming from overhead, picked out the natural lights of her hair. At the door she turned with a friendly smile. "Well, good-bye again, Marshall," she said with a lightness he knew assumed. The words sounded so conclusive, so awesomely final that he could not resist relieving the moment by briefly touching

121

his lips to her cheek. But she turned toward him as he bent his head, and he found himself staring into her eyes. Hers dropped to his lips as if wondering where they had sprung from, the gesture so bewitchingly provocative and innocent at the same time that he reached out, his hand finding the small of her back, and drew her against his chest. "Marshall," she said in surprise, her lips opening like a petal to form his name as he bent his head.

He meant only to kiss her fully, then take his leave and be damned to all the Kingstons. But her mouth moved beneath his, and he tasted a seductiveness of flesh that he had never known before. His senses leaped, his arms tightened. He pressed her into him, aching with a new and deeper need than any he had ever felt.

"Aly," he whispered between a grin and a groan when he'd released her mouth.

"The stick-figure kid herself," she assured him softly, her mouth moist, her eyes shining.

"No, not any longer." Tenderly he cradled her face in his hands. Moonlight glimmered in her eyes, glistened off her teeth, flooded her face with an unimaginable beauty. He could have cried from the loss that filled his soul. "You have become irresistible, Aly Kingston. It is possible you could break my heart."

"Oh, I'd never do that, Marshall Wayne. I would be the best keeper of your heart imaginable."

He lowered his head to kiss her again before she could see the quick spring of sorrow in his eyes, and Aly kissed him back, her lips unreserved and full of promise.

"Now," Marshall said afterward, taking a deep breath, "this is my advice to you. I think you'd better let me go, or I won't, if you catch my meaning."

Aly smiled seductively, keeping her arms around his waist,

nuzzling his earlobe. "It was your idea to go in the first place, you may remember."

"Aly." Resolutely, Marshall set her from him. Again, the moonlight fell on her face, and his breath caught. He cleared his throat. "About this riding business," he began. "Don't you find it a little embarrassing that you don't know how to ride?"

"Nobody knows but you and Joe and Willy. I've managed to keep the fact a secret." Aly yearned to have him stay. Forever and ever.

"Well, look," he said gruffly, fingertips going back into his pockets, "if you don't have any plans tomorrow night, I'll come out and give you your first lesson. I promised it to you, and I never break my promise."

The hard fact of his last statement broke the spell between them. For a fraction of a second their glances locked, then Marshall's skewed away. His handsome face closed. Aly suddenly thought of the white Continental. There had not been a rental sticker anywhere on it. He must own the car and had arranged to have it delivered to Oklahoma City. But it didn't matter. So what? Marshall would be back tomorrow night. She had won this first round.

"Will six o'clock be all right with you?" Aly asked. "And how about supper afterward here at the house?"

"Suits me," he said. He did not touch her again, but opened the door and stepped out onto the porch. At the bottom of the steps he looked back up at her standing in the doorway. "By the way," he said, "thanks for planting the geraniums."

"You're welcome, Marshall."

At his motel, Marshall stepped out onto the veranda of his upper floor room, lighting a fresh cigarette. The burning sensation was back in his chest. Before he got back to the motel, because

123

he would have had to go through a switchboard there, he tried Hattie Handlin's number and received no answer. Claiborne folks, even for a Saturday night, were usually in bed by now. He could only deduce that Hattie was out of town.

Tomorrow he would drive by her house. His presence in the neighborhood would rouse no suspicions. He was merely out on a nostalgic drive through the residential sections of his home-town. Maybe he could find out something. Right now he must try not to worry over something that might have a perfectly harmless explanation. Hattie could have gone to see a sick rela-tive. Rather than trust anyone with a message, she had decided to wait until she got back to get in touch with him, knowing that he would be here for several weeks. After all, there was plenty of time for their transaction.

He drew deeply on the cigarette, staring out toward Cedar Hill. Aly, though, might be a problem he hadn't counted on. He still felt the warm imprint of her body, the responding pressure of her lips. She had felt so good in his arms, and it had been an effort to let her go. The next time he might not be able to.

Aly walked out onto the porch at Cedar Hill, glad of the night wind that blew through her hair, cooling the fever that Marshall had kindled. He was staying in the new motel on the other side of town, he had said. She gazed in its direction, hugging herself to keep the contact of him with her awhile longer. What was the "something else" in his life that he could not share? Could she displace it, she wondered.

Even as she thought it, the light wind ran caressing fingers over her body, reminding her of Marshall. She shuddered deli-ciously. Well, she certainly intended to try.

Chapter Nine

Marshall Wayne credited much of his financial success to the near infallibility of his instincts. The next morning as he drove slowly by Hattie Handlin's trim, modest bungalow, this set of faculties told him that the final phase of his carefully planned scheme was in trouble. Hattie's ancient Chevrolet was in the carport, but the yellowing newspapers in the front yard indicated that she had not been home for several days. Where the hell had the woman gone to?

She was to have been waiting for him on Friday to sell him her shares in the Kingston State Bank, a purchase that would put him in control of fifty-one percent of the stock. Even more important was the proxy letter she had agreed to give him authorizing him to vote her shares in the stockholders' meeting next week. For though he would own the stock, his name would not be on the current list of stockholders eligible to cast a ballot in the reelection of the board of directors. The list was compiled twenty days in advance of the meeting. Those not on the list would have to wait until next year to vote. Marshall had no intention of waiting. He had come to depose Lorne Kingston this year.

But he had to have that letter. Surely Hattie hadn't changed her mind or been approached by Lorne Kingston with a better offer? Alarm shot through him at the possibility, quickly discarded. The old reprobate couldn't possibly know of his intent, and Hattie Handlin hated Kingston as much as he did. She was still smarting from the snub given her nephew by Victoria years ago. Little old ladies like Hattie did not forgive arrogant young ladies like Victoria easily. Also, shortly after Hattie was widowed, Lorne Kingston had approached her about investing her insurance money in something guaranteed to provide her with a financially secure old age: Kingston State Bank stock. He had even offered to sell her some of his own personal shares. The rest of the story was history. "It'll be a pleasure to let you have the shares, Marshall." Hattie had smacked with malice over the phone when he had called with his offer. "I figure I know why you want 'em, and I'm countin' on you to put a certain Mr. Big Shot in his place. You just give me a call when you get into town. I'll be waiting."

Marshall wondered if Hattie had told Joe about their negotiations. She had promised not to. He wanted no one at this point to know about his purchase of the shares. By not buying them until after the twenty-day period, his name would not appear on the stockholders list. As far as anybody knew, Marshall Wayne did not own or control a single share. By the time he showed his hand, it would be too late for Lorne Kingston to stop him.

But also, Marshall had to admit, part of his pleasure in dethroning Kingston and ruining his son's expectations of being named president and chairman when his father retired next month was the surprise he anticipated seeing on their faces when he walked into that meeting and presented Hattie's letter. By then the proxy ballots of the forty-one percent of the shares he controlled would have been counted and their negative results known. All would have registered against retaining the current board. He relished the mental picture of the shocked reactions when the Kingstons and the board realized they were out. In the general business meeting following, he, as majority stockholder, would then nominate a new board, men he knew would agree to serve, and they in turn would elect him president and chairman. God, what a sweet victory! But he had to have that letter.

Coming up the street was a white pickup. As the two vehicles drew abreast, Marshall stiffened as he saw the logo of Green Meadows on the door, then looked up at the face of the driver. Joe Handlin's green eyes widened in recognition, and he motioned Marshall to pull over. The pickup backed up alongside the Lincoln, and Joe rolled his window down. "Well, hello there, Marshall," he said. "I heard you were back in town. What are you doing in this neighborhood? Anything I can help you with?"

Marshall listened for anything in the tone or words to indicate that Joe knew the answer to that question. "Just driving around town," he answered. "It doesn't seem to have changed much. Your aunt still live on this block?"

"Yeah. She's been wanting to move to an apartment, someplace smaller, ever since Uncle Rupert died. Wants me to rent the place from her, but I can't do that. I live out close to Green Meadows so I can be near Aly if she needs me." This last information was dropped pointedly, in a way that made Marshall think it was for his benefit. He filed it away for later.

"How is your aunt, by the way? She must be nearing seventy by now."

"Not so good, I'm afraid. She had a severe heart attack last week and has been in intensive care at the hospital ever since. I've come by this morning to pick up her mail and the newspapers in the yard. Open invitation to burglars."

Marshall kept his expression of polite concern and interest

firmly in place. "I'm sorry to hear that," he said. "What are her chances of making it?"

"Pretty slim. I've been trying to get used to the idea. She and Uncle Rupert raised me when my folks died, you remember."

"I remember. I'm sorry, Joe."

The two men drove off with a wave, but green eyes and brown ones surveyed each other in sideview mirrors. As classmates, the two men had never been particularly friendly, but they had respected each other. Joe had his cap set for Aly, Marshall surmised, and the man saw him as a threat to his hopes. He would concern himself about that later. Right now he had to concentrate on what he would do if Hattie Handlin died before he got his hands on her proxy letter.

"That doesn't look suitable for riding," Marshall said, appraising the dusky blue blouse and skirt Aly was wearing. She stood framed in the doorway of her house, the subdued light of the breezeway glowing softly on her hair. "You're not trying to get out of that riding lesson, are you?"

"Not at all, Marshall." Actually, until the phone call from Joe, she had thought of nothing else all day unless it was the meal she had painstakingly prepared. "I'm sorry, but our plans have changed," she explained. "I tried to get you at the motel, but you were out. My stable manager's aunt is at the hospital near death. I thought I ought to be with him right now. Willy is there, too."

Aly saw something like a shock wave pass over the well-cut features. Now that she looked at Marshall closer, she thought she detected signs of strain about his eyes. Had he been battling with himself about coming here this evening? "Do you mind if I come with you?" Marshall asked. "I remember Joe Handlin."

"I was hoping you would want to." She smiled. "Come in while I get my jacket."

At the hospital they found Joe and Willy in the waiting room reserved for the family of patients in the intensive care unit. Joe's face fell visibly when he saw Marshall, and he took Aly's hands possessively, pulling her aside for a private conference. "Thanks for coming, hon. I don't think Aunt Hattie can last much longer." He cast a glance at Marshall. "I appreciate you bringing Aly out, Marshall. I'll see that she gets home."

"Aly and I had a date tonight. I'll see that she gets home," Marshall stated quietly.

Willy moved into the tense moment with a placid comment that prevented the discussion from getting out of hand. Soon Hattie's family began to arrive from neighboring counties. "See the vultures gathering," Joe remarked uncharitably, sighting the first group coming down the hall. "They all think Aunt Hattie remembered them in her will, but I know she didn't. She left everything to me." He looked directly at Marshall as he spoke. "Everything. The house, some bonds, a few shares of stock...I think I'll hold on to the stock. I see no reason to sell it. No reason at all."

Aly looked from one to the other, reading a secret communication between the two men, sensing their hostility. Why was Joe discussing Hattie's will almost within earshot of her deathbed? Joe adored his aunt and would have been satisfied with just the memory of the love and attention she'd showered on him through the years. She saw Marshall's jaw go rigid. "One thing about stock," he said. "If you hold it too long, the price could go down."

"Sometimes their value isn't counted in dollars."

The arrival of Joe's relatives prevented further discussion. As greetings and news of Hattie's condition were exchanged, Marshall gripped Aly's arm. "Let's get out of here as soon as we can," he ordered in a low tone.

"I can't, Marshall. Joe needs me."

"I need you more. He has his family."

Hattie died an hour later, and soon after the news came Marshall shepherded Aly out of the hospital. "You're upset," she declared, "and it isn't because of Hattie's death. What's the matter, Marshall? What was going on back there between you and Joe?"

"Nothing. The guy's in love with you. He thinks I'm here to shoot him out of the saddle."

Don't I wish, she threw back mentally, but asked, "What's that got to do with stocks?"

"Oh, that was just a play on words between us men, honey. Didn't mean a thing. Where can we go for a bite to eat?"

"Back to the house," she said, disarmed by the endearment and remembering his statement to her back at the hospital. *I need you more.* That had a nice ring to it. "I have supper ready to pop into the oven," she said. "Fricasseed chicken. Hattie would want us to enjoy it."

Marshall dragged his eyes away from the road where they had been focused in severe thought. The distracted smile he gave her did little to convince Aly of his interest in the meal. "Fricasseed chicken, huh? With rice?"

"And apple salad and pecan pie for dessert."

"Sounds like one of Mother's meals."

"It should. She taught me all I know about cooking—the recipes are hers."

"Great!" he said with a heartiness that did not quite ring true. Aly observed him out of the corner of her eye. What was happening here all of a sudden? What had that exchange been about back at the hospital? She guessed she'd just get Joe to tell her.

* * *

In the parlor, while Aly put the finishing touches on their meal, Marshall roamed about like a caged animal, stopping every now and then to draw on the cigarette that he had lighted without thinking. How in hell could he rectify this unforeseen set of events? Why hadn't he thought of this possibility earlier and bought Hattie's stock sooner? The voice of logic reminded him that to have done so might have tipped his hand to Lorne, who could have exercised any number of options to block the takeover. Calmly he considered the facts. Joe Handlin knew about his arrangement to buy Hattie's stock, that was certain. What else did he know or guess? How much had Hattie told him? Marshall conjectured that the attack may have hit her before the proxy letter had been written. Realizing she could be dying, she had told Joe about the shares, possibly instructed him to sell as agreed. But Joe had no intention of selling him those shares now, and if they were sold to Lorne Kingston, who might very well make Joe an offer now that Hattie was dead, then the dream to remove Kingston and take over the bank was finished. Unless he could get his hands on another ten percent, his shrewd accumulation of the stock would be worthless, and a costly, all-consuming ambition that had been the purpose of his life for thirteen years would be down the drain. But where was he to get it?

"Marshall?" Aly called from the doorway between the parlor and dining room. "Supper's on the table."

He turned to her slowly, fixing her with a gaze dark and considering. Aly marked the cigarette, the odd expression, the aloofness of his manner with a chill of apprehension along her spine. "Marshall?" she asked quizzically, in the tone of one identifying a stranger.

He blinked, then smiled, connecting them again. He noticed the cigarette. "Sorry," he said, stubbing it out in the one ashtray in the parlor. "I have the feeling you don't approve of these."

"You didn't either before."

"That was before."

They had just sat down at the table when the doorbell rang.

"Who the hell is that?" Marshall demanded with unwonted feeling.

"I'll go see."

It was Joe. Through the oval glass, Aly could see him standing impatiently under the illumination of the porch light, casting malevolent glances at the Lincoln Continental. His eyes looked red-rimmed and swollen.

"Hello, Aly," he said when she opened the door. "I'm glad to see you're still up and dressed." He pushed back his cap nervously.

"Why shouldn't I be, Joe?" she said. "It's only eight-thirty."

"Marshall here?"

"Yes."

"Can I talk to you?"

"Certainly. Come in."

"No. I mean out here."

"Joe," Aly tried to keep her voice gentle, but what was he doing here? He ought to be in church or with his relatives or seeing to funeral arrangements—anywhere but here, keeping a birdwatch on her and Marshall at such a time. "Anything you want to say to me can be said inside. Marshall is my guest. It's rude to talk out here."

"It's about Marshall that I've come."

Aly pulled the door shut behind her. "What about him?"

"He's up to something, Aly. I'm not exactly sure what, but it has to do with Aunt Hattie's Kingston State Bank stock. He came here to buy it. She told me so herself just before the ambulance came to take her to the hospital."

Aly received this information calmly, though its impact was

like a blow to her stomach. "So?" she said, keeping her tone mild. "What has that got to do with me?"

Alarmed at her attitude, Joe struggled to keep his voice down. "Well, doesn't that bother you, Aly? Doesn't that tell you something? I figure Marshall wants that stock in order to gain control of your father's bank somehow."

Aly's mind was working fast, adding up certain expressions, comments, feelings, facts noted and learned in the last few days. The sum appalled her only a little less than her own stupidity. So Marshall had not come to buy Cedar Hill. He had come for Hattie's stocks. She should have realized that fact when they were mentioned at the hospital. Their loss explained the look that had been on Marshall's face, his distraction during the drive home. It explained that strange expression he had turned to her when she called him in to supper. Dear God! Now that Hattie's stock had fallen through the crack, did that mean he intended to come after hers?

Aly transferred her attention to Joe. Until she could get a handle on this, she had to do something about Joe. His curiosity, if not extinguished now, could spread like a brush fire. He would question and probe and dig until he unearthed answers satisfactory to his resourceful intelligence. Also, she had to prevent him from selling those shares—either to Marshall or her father.

Though she already knew, Aly asked, "How many shares did your aunt own?" When Joe cited the number, she said, "That represents only ten percent, Joe, not enough to give Marshall much clout even if he did own them. They would have to be combined with others to give him the needed majority to oust my father."

Joe, all perked ears now, asked narrowly, "Exactly how does that work?"

"Well, to remove my father as chairman, a new board of directors opposed to him would have to be elected. That would come about only if those owning the majority of stock, fifty-one percent, voted to oust the old board and elect a new one. Only the board of directors can hire or fire a chairman."

"So that means that if Marshall owned fifty-one percent of the stock, he could sweep the board clean all by himself."

"That's right, but he doesn't. He doesn't possess a single share, according to the annual stockholders' report."

"Then why the hell would he want to buy Aunt Hattie's measly ten percent?"

Aly shrugged. "You got me. Maybe just to be a thorn in Dad's side at the stockholders' meetings the way Aunt Hattie has been for years. Marshall came to Claiborne to buy Cedar Hill from Matt, you know."

At Joe's look of surprise, she grinned. "He didn't know that I had bought it."

Joe returned the grin with satisfaction. "Looks like that boy is being cut off at the pass from every direction. So you think he thought that since he'd have a claim in Claiborne again, he'd just buy himself a seat in the meetings with Aunt Hattie's shares?"

"That's what I think, Joe. I'd just hold on to that stock if I were you. The bank's turning around. Those shares may become a very valuable asset one of these days."

Joe settled his cap down over the pale green eyes decisively. "I'm satisfied," he said, "but I got one more question to ask you, Aly. Why is he hanging around—you being a Kingston and all?"

"I think he thinks I may be persuaded to sell Cedar Hill."

"And what form might that persuasion take?"

"You're getting a little personal now, Joe."

"Well then, answer me this. Could you be persuaded to sell Cedar Hill?"

"You know the answer to that, friend." Aly allowed a conspiratorial glint to appear in her eye, relieved to see Joe's slow, acknowledging grin.

"That's my girl," he said. "Now, you think you could do without me for about a week? I got so many things that need doing right now—"

"I insist that you take next week off, Joe," Aly said commiseratively, seeing the wash of sorrow back in his eyes. Moved by compassion for him, she pressed her hand to his cheek. "Take as long as you need. Willy and I can manage."

He squeezed her hand in response, then kissed its palm. "Don't manage too well," he said.

When he was gone, Aly went back inside, pausing briefly in the breezeway to collect her thoughts. She hadn't lied to Joe. She had simply not told him the whole truth. She had not explained that to oust a chairman of the board, a stockholder did not have to *own* fifty-one percent of the shares. He merely had to *control* them. The only reason Marshall would have sought Hattie's shares, had come at this time to buy them, was because he already controlled forty-one percent. What, she wondered, growing cold, would be his next move?

"Your dinner is probably cold," Marshall commented in annoyance when she took her place at the table. "Who was that?"

"Joe Handlin," she said, in case he had come to check on her and saw him on the porch. "One of the boys" would have been a suspicious evasion. Her body felt numb.

"What did he want?"

"A week off. I gave it to him. He needs it."

Marshall had waited for her to begin the meal. Now he cut into a chicken breast with what she knew to be feigned en-

135

thusiasm, took a bite, and chewed blissfully. "Excellent," he pronounced.

"I hope this meal won't provoke painful memories," Aly said, keeping her eyes on her plate and taking her time in slicing her own portion.

"Not at all. I'm glad Mother's culinary talents live on in you, Aly. I'm glad so much of what I cared for lives on in you, as a matter of fact." He underscored the sentiment with a devastating smile, emptying her heart. When she did not respond, he paused from his eating, watching her. "Anything the matter?"

She looked up, eyes innocent. "Joe's on my mind, I guess. It will be hard on him for a while with his aunt gone."

Marshall went back to his fricasseed chicken. "You'll be shorthanded with Joe gone," he said. "How about letting me fill in for him until he comes back?"

Aly's head popped up. "You mean *work* here at Green Meadows?"

"Why not? I'd very much like to help you out."

"But—but this is your vacation."

"I can't think of a better way to spend it. You know, Aly, it crossed my mind when I was growing up to turn Cedar Hill into a horse breeding farm someday. Don't look so surprised. I thought Mother would have told you. Sampson was my first purchase toward that possible goal. I'd enjoy working around here for the next week. What with Sampson here and Willy and the house—and you—I'd feel almost home again."

How warm and winning the words sounded. They were what she wanted to hear, and he probably knew it, but were they the truth? Was his offer genuinely extended to help her out, or was it a pretext made to give him the opportunity to seduce her shares from her? She would have to wait and see. She was no longer sure of him, of Sy and Elizabeth's son.

Then, as she considered him, a notion so stunning, so unbelievable, so absolutely right, smacked her with such force that she was obliged to cough delicately into her napkin. *So what if Marshall's motives might be less than honorable*, she asked herself. *Why not give him reason to change his mind—his heart! Why not give him reason to abandon this whole ridiculous idea of taking over the Kingston State Bank! Take the offensive!* That had always been her father's favorite dictum in business and in that respect at least, she had proved to be his daughter.

So why not take it now? Why not go after Marshall, seduce him? *Why not woo him, win him, keep him here forever! He belonged in Claiborne. He belonged on Cedar Hill with her. He just thought he wanted to become president and chairman of the Kingston State Bank. What he really wanted was to marry her and help her run Green Meadows.*

Taking a sip of water to clear her throat, Aly set down the glass and smiled, completely restored. "It's a deal," she said. "Can you start in the morning?"

They decided to clear away the dishes before having pie and coffee on the porch. In the kitchen Aly hummed while Marshall carried in the dishes from the living room. He studied her covertly, in an anguish to know if Joe Handlin had spilled the beans about the shares. From Aly's cheerful manner, he decided that Joe, not understanding their actual importance to him, had not. Maybe he had been too broken up over his aunt's death to mention them.

Did Aly ever read the bank's annual report? Did she know or care that her family no longer held a majority of the stock? She could not possibly know whose hand controlled forty-one percent of the outstanding shares. But did she suspect? And if Joe told her later about his offer to buy Hattie's ten percent, which she knew wouldn't be honored now, then what would she deduce?

A feeling of loss swept through him, a melancholia that sent him to stand behind Aly and wrap his arms around her. He kissed the top of her head. "Just think, a whole week together. A whole anything-could-happen week."

"You said it," Aly said. "This is the tornado season, you know, so I'm doubly appreciative of your offer, Marshall. I usually try to hire extra men this time of year simply to help us round up the mares and foals in the pastures when we get the warnings, but temporary help is hard to come by. I have no trouble when school is out because I can hire teenagers, but right now—"

"Is that all you're thinking about—how much help I can be? I had other things in mind, too."

Still in his arms, she turned around to face him, the movement alluring and feminine, igniting his desire. Her eyes were wide and quizzical. "But, Marshall, I thought—last night you said—"

He slipped his hand up through her hair and drew her to him. "That was last night," he said roughly. "I haven't been able to get you out of my mind, Aly." *It was true*, he thought, as he covered her mouth. Her lips parted. He could feel the sensuous touch of her hands finding their way around his neck. She moved against him, whether consciously, he could not tell. All he knew was that she was drawing him away on some sea of passion, or feeling, heretofore uncharted in his experience. His last awareness before he found himself opening the door of his old room to lead her inside was to ponder the two questions of how could he live with what he was about to do and how could he live without it.

Chapter Ten

Aly's built-in alarm woke her at the usual time Monday morning. For a few blissful minutes she lay on her back, letting herself slowly come awake to the memory of the night before. Then, without opening her eyes, she reached over to the other side of the bed to feel for substantial evidence that it had not all been a dream. Her hand fell upon empty bedsheets.

"Marshall?" she exclaimed, sitting up in surprise. She listened for sounds of him in the adjoining bathroom, and when none came, she hurriedly threw back the covers and pushed into a pair of slippers by the bedside. Drawing on a robe, she went down the breezeway to the kitchen.

He had gone. A note by the coffeepot explained, in an endearingly prudish fashion, that he thought it wise his car not be discovered in front of her house should one of her men show up there Monday morning. "Claiborne isn't New York, you know," he wrote, saying that he had gone to the motel and would be back out to Green Meadows after breakfast.

Aly put the coffeepot on and went out onto the porch to wait for it to perk. She sat down on the couch and drew her robe around her, snuggling into it as she thought with sublime satisfaction that some realities were better than dreams ever could be. He was right about the car, of course, but if she'd known

Marshall would be gone when she awoke, she doubted if she would have slept.

All night long she had marveled at the miracle of his presence beside her. And because it was a miracle, then that meant it was supposed to be. It was just that simple. Marshall would fall in love with her, go back to New York to resign his position (if he hadn't already), and then return to Claiborne to marry her. They would reside on Cedar Hill and live happily ever after. She wasn't one to put much stock in fantasies, but she did believe in miracles.

Oh, Marshall would have a struggle on his hands right now, she could appreciate that. How confused he must be this morning, how frustrated to know she was his only hope to accomplish what he'd set out to do thirteen years ago. And to be so close...Now he'd have to decide whether his hate for her father outweighed his growing love for her. And she knew it was love. There had been something so tender, so genuine in his awe of her, his feeling for her, something so beyond what he had expected from both of them for the night to have been called anything but an expression of love.

She would have to give him time to come around. In the meantime, she wouldn't give him the minutest reason to believe she was on to him, that she knew why he had come to Claiborne, why he'd offered to fill in for Joe, why he'd made love to her—and might again before he called off this whole thing with her father. And he would call it off. She knew Sy and Elizabeth's son. Come time for the board meeting in eight days, Marshall Wayne would not be attending.

Marshall walked out of Willard's Cafe where he had just had breakfast into the sunshine of a fresh spring morning. Skies were blue, the breeze was gentle, the air invigorating, but he took no notice of any of these end-of-winter beneficences that as a boy on his morning chores had made his family's farm the finest place in the world to be. His chest felt so tight that the mitigation of a deep breath wasn't worth the pain of it. He yearned to take a swing at something, anything good and solid, but preferably the jaw of Lorne Kingston. Damn, if it wasn't for him, how different everything would be! How simple and uncomplicated—how beautiful.

How, he demanded in frustration as he lit a cigarette, had everything skittered so far off track? Five days ago when he stepped off that plane in Oklahoma City, everything he needed to destroy Lorne Kingston was in the bag. Nobody but that double-dealing conniver stood to get hurt, not even Lorne Junior, who, for the first time in his life, could get his backside out of that bank and go to work like other men's sons.

But now Aly was involved, and the last thing he wanted was to hurt her. Unbidden, before he could stop it, the memory of her in his arms last night flooded over him. He saw her face gazing up at him, her head pillowed on the golden cushion of her hair. Unable to stanch them, he felt again the desires that had put all others out of his mind, that had made him loath to leave her in the early hours of the morning before she could wake and make him stay.

Marshall cursed under his breath. What an ironic turn of events. It would be only a matter of time before Aly found out that he'd made Hattie an offer for her stock. Joe would have every reason to tell her. He might even go to her father with the information, who wouldn't waste a panicky second informing Aly.

And what then?

Marshall took a deep draw on the cigarette, feeling the acrid smoke burn a trail to his lungs. In disgust he looked at it, then flicked it into the street. Aly was right. He hadn't liked them before. He didn't now. A motorist, his face friendly and familiar, waved at him. Marshall waved back, feeling his chest loosen somewhat. It was good to stand here in the peace and quiet of morning and be hailed by old friends. Quite a contrast from New York. He would be going back now, all that he'd come home for—and more besides—lost to him once again.

He began to walk. Up the block was the Kingston State Bank. He had been avoiding it as he had been avoiding the sight of Lorne Kingston. He had not wanted to lay eyes on him until the day of the board meeting. He hoped the old boy still stood tall and straight, still had that superior way of looking over his glasses at you as if you'd asked to go to the bathroom in his house. He wanted no reason to feel sorry for him, no reason later to regret what he'd done. But now he wanted to see him. He wanted a look at the bank.

Marshall crossed the street and sauntered down the sidewalk until he drew abreast of the bank on the other side. Then, slipping his fingers into the top of his jeans pockets, he stood there looking at it, imagining the name Kingston removed from the sign and himself as president and chairman. Wayne State Bank. It could still be his. That was the biggest irony of all. If he chose, it could still be his.

His glance sharpened as two men, one old, one young, pushed open the double glass doors from inside the bank. Lorne Kingston and his son. Lorne Junior was heavier than when Marshall had last seen him, but his father, though completely gray now, was still trim and suave. He still walked with that arrogant air of self-esteem that Marshall had looked forward to extinguishing. As he watched their progress down the street, observed the deference they were accorded, hate surged anew within him. How quickly people forgot. The ruined acres of

Cedar Hill, which had lain exposed to public scrutiny for at least three years, were evidence of what Lorne Kingston could do to people like the Waynes. Yet he and his son could still be treated with respect, slapped on the back, and welcomed into the coffee klatch of local businessmen and farmers that gathered about now at Willard's.

Marshall, his thirst for vengeance fully returned, watched as Mrs. Devers—grayer, a bit stooped, but amazingly fast on her feet—rushed out of the bank in pursuit of the two Kingstons. At once Marshall became interested in the window display behind him. In the glass he saw the pair turn at the cry of their names and wait for the excited woman. They conferred, then in alarm all three hurried back and reentered the bank.

Marshall smiled, welcoming the surge of pleasure through his bitterness like a draught of fresh air in a stale room. He started back down the street toward his car. Temporarily at least, he had thrown a rock into the spokes of the biggest wheel in town.

In the breezeway, Aly was just hanging up the phone when she saw Marshall coming up the steps. Today he wore a western straw hat, an addition to the jeans and boots, which she thought made his true image complete. She stayed in her chair, watching him reflect a moment on a pot of geraniums, then go back down the steps. Afraid that he might be leaving, she hastened to the door, but was cautioned by some instinct to peep through the glass first. Marshall was making for the pecan trees, his long-legged stride recalling another time when she followed him down the steps in beseeching pursuit. She watched him stop in the shade of the newly budded limbs, their shadows gamboling over him in merry play. What was he thinking, standing there like that in the stance of men whose lives are spent in con-

143

stant surveillance of crops and animals and weather? What was Marshall surveying? The yesterdays of Cedar Hill? The succession of seasons and cornfields and the secondhand vehicles once parked between the trees?

Aly thought she knew. She had just spoken with her father. He had sounded out of breath, for he had just run from Willard's to the bank after Mrs. Devers had gone to tell him the results of the first proxy forms. All had voted against retaining the board.

"My God, I can't believe the finesse, the years involved in this! He's out to get us, Alyson. I'm convinced that all those proxies will come in negative now that I've learned Marshall came here to buy Hattie Handlin's shares—"

"Did he?" she asked calmly.

"You know he did! Joe told me so himself when I called him at the funeral home minutes ago. I offered to buy Hattie's shares. But he won't sell to me—says he's not selling to anybody, which means Marshall can't get his hands on them either. Now, Aly, you're his only prayer for getting the ten percent he needs. I know he'll try to fleece your shares out of you. He's started already if I'm to believe Joe. But I'm telling you that if you're fool enough to let him, the family will disown you. You'll never set foot in this house again. I'll keep Peter from you—"

"You can forget the threats, Dad," she had cut in. "I'm not about to sell my shares to Marshall Wayne. I wouldn't do such a thing to him." She had hung up, leaving her father still on the line trying to figure out her last remark.

But what would she do if Marshall asked her for the shares? Watching him come back to the house, his face drawn from the struggle within him, she had a moment of panic. She knew what her answer would be, but Lord, what would she *do*! How could she order him out of her life? How could she live the rest of it with the memory that for a while, a precious, beautiful while, he had been such an intimate part of it?

But he wouldn't ask her for those shares, she decided resolutely, opening the door, her smile ready and welcoming. Miracles never went awry.

"Good morning!" she greeted him happily. "Why so glum, chum? Having second thoughts about working during your vacation?"

"Not about that."

"About last night then?" she asked, sweeping off his hat as he gathered her to him.

"No," he said, holding her as if she'd been about to fall. "Never about last night. Never, never about last night."

The day went fast with barely enough time to eat the sandwiches Aly had packed for Marshall and Willy and herself for lunch. Almost hourly a horse trailer or van arrived either to deliver or pick up their valuable cargoes. Marshall, with the instinctive understanding of a born horseman, took charge of loading and unloading the stock. Calm and patient, he was able to soothe the crankiest of the travelers in the tricky process of leading them from vehicle to paddock where stiff legs and tempers could be run off.

Gratefully, Aly left Marshall to the chores she would have had to see after in Joe's absence and devoted her time to the necessary paperwork and entertainment of her visitors. She was even able to take time to slip into town to pay her last respects to Hattie at the funeral home, where she unfortunately had an ugly encounter with Joe.

"I hear Marshall Wayne is my temporary relief."

"News travels fast."

"That surprise you in this town? He going to fill in the full week?"

"Yes."

"So I guess it's lucky for you that I had to be off this week."

"He offered to help out, and I'm grateful for it, Joe. That's all there is to it."

"You know, your dad made me a pretty tempting offer this morning. I've been thinking about it, and the more I think about it, the more tempting it seems. Especially if it means cutting Marshall's legs right out from under him. Know the offer I'm talking about?"

"I know, Joe. Here's mine. If you sell those shares to my father before the board meeting next Tuesday, you will never get another job with a major horsebreeding operation in this state."

"It's that way, is it?"

"It's that way. Leave it be, Joe. You made the right decision when you told my father no this morning. Let it ride now."

That evening, accompanying her on the nightly tour of the stables, Marshall asked, "Tired?"

"Not as much as you are, I'd bet. You've had a long day."

"I've enjoyed every minute of it. I can't remember when I've enjoyed a day more, but I could sure use a beer when we get up to the house."

"You got it. Want to stay for supper?"

"I ought to take you out."

She laughed at his unenthusiasm. "I put on a roast awhile ago, hoping you'd stay. No need to go back to the motel to change. You can wash up at the house."

In the bathroom, Marshall finished drying his face and hands and looked at himself in the mirror. The first of the proxies had arrived today. He had ordered that they come in a trickle, all negative, with the last of them delivered the day before the meeting. He wanted to draw out Kingston's pain, make him sweat and worry. It had been an excellent plan. By now he was to have had Hattie's proxy letter. He could go out on the porch in a moment, accept a beer from Aly, sit down at her supper, and never feel a pang. After all, he'd made it clear long ago how he felt about her father, what he hoped to do, how his white Continental would someday be parked in the president's spot at the bank.

But now—now everything had changed. His lips twisted wryly. So much for the dramatic point of the white Continental. His stomach had never felt tied in so many knots. He kept waiting for the phone to ring. It could be Joe or it could be her father, both with news that would make Aly fix him with a look in a moment that said she knew his motives for last night, for today, for the rest of the week.

He looked long at his face in the mirror. He had always accepted without the least conceit that his looks could lead women to make fools of themselves. But not Aly. Aly was the kind of woman who, once one of those calls came through, would be able to say to him what long ago he had said to her. He could never come back then, never come home again.

He sighed, hanging the towel neatly over the rack attached to the same spot as the one he'd known years ago. This was what it was like to feel old, he thought.

She handed him a beer when he joined her on the back porch. A table had been set for two at the far end, and the savory aroma of roast beef drifted in from the kitchen. The jalousied windows had been rolled out, and the porch was redolent with the smells of rich earth and spring grass. Below, the panorama of Green Meadows stretched out under the silver light of a full moon.

"You look delicious," he said, taking the beer. She had changed into a long colorfully embroidered caftan in yellow cotton and tied a narrow ribbon in the same shade around her hair.

"Thank you." Aly smiled. "I'll put on some records in a minute. Right now I want to hear the weather news. One of the trainers said that a tornado had been sighted near Oklahoma City."

"Have you ever had any damage from tornadoes here at Green Meadows?" Marshall asked, taking a seat on the couch and resting his arm on the back. He could hardly take his eyes off her.

"No, and we're long overdue. Our luck can't hold forever. I just hope we have all the visiting stock out of here when one of those rip-snorters heads this way. Our own animals know us, and we won't have any trouble leading them to the barns."

Marshall drank his beer, observing her golden head bent close to the small radio on the bookshelf. Her expression was intense as she listened, and he thought with admiration what a great place she had here, how orderly and prosperous. The men thought highly of her, obvious from the way they discussed her every remark and action with respect and affection. Despair pushed deep in his chest, and he fought the urge for a cigarette. Damn you, Hattie Handlin! Why'd you have to die?

Aly turned off the weather news, flicked on the stereo. "Anything you'd like?" she asked.

"Are we speaking of records?"

She threw a pillow from a nearby chair at him. "Yes." She laughed. "At least for now."

"You choose."

She stacked a selection of instrumentals on the turntable, then joined him on the couch with a glass of wine. "This is nice. This is the time of day when it's good to be with someone. I'm glad you're here, Marshall."

"No happier than I am," he said, realizing how much he meant it. He pulled a little away from her, wanting nothing more than to draw nearer, to lose himself in all that clean shining wholesomeness, to kiss her hard enough to feel the ridge of those straightened little teeth. He got up abruptly to stroll over to the windows for a better view of the night vista of Green Meadows.

From the couch, Aly watched him. *He doesn't know what to do about this evening*, she said to herself. *He's battling with his conscience about whether he should stay. If he's falling in love with me, he won't. If he's still after those shares, he will.* Who would win out by evening's end? The man who had come to depose her father or the man she loved as Sy and Elizabeth's boy? She knew on whom she'd put her money. But, goodness, she would miss him tonight!

Dinner was saved from being an awkward affair by Aly pretending not to notice. Taking pity on Marshall's plight, she kept her distance from him and conversed lightly about matters of the day.

"Let me help you with those," he offered when the meal came to an end and Aly got up to take their plates into the kitchen.

"If you like," she said. She hung back to allow Marshall to precede her into the kitchen. Then, brushing by a bookcase next to the door, her long dress somehow caught the edge of a scrap book. Down it went on its face, jostling out contents that Aly had purposefully loosened earlier in the day.

"How clumsy of me," she bemoaned, in what she thought a convincing tone, as Marshall returned from the kitchen. Hands full, she stood looking down helplessly at the fragile, timeworn album in danger of spine damage.

"I'll get it," he said, kneeling down to pick up the book and collect the snapshots and clippings. Aly remained until his attention caught, then left him poring over the material in fascination.

When she brought in their coffee and pecan pie after an interval she judged sufficient to her designs, Marshall was sitting on the couch thoroughly immersed in the contents. He looked up wonderingly, nostalgia soft in his eyes. "Where did you get all these?" he marveled, holding up a number of photographs of himself and his parents at Cedar Hill.

"Don't you remember when I used to follow you around with my camera? Probably not," she said reminiscently. "But in those days I took so many pictures that the snap of my shutter and the pop of my flash were about as common as the sound of cowbells."

"Apparently so, from the number of these pictures," Marshall mused. "And the clippings! You must have cut out everything ever written about me."

"Which ought to give you some idea of the extent of the crush I had on you," Aly pointed out saucily. Her eye had an impish gleam.

"Fortunate for me that you didn't leave it in the past along with your camera," he said. He looked again through the photographs. "I'm grateful that you took these, Aly. I'd like to have some reprints made from them if you don't mind. I have very few keepsakes from Cedar Hill. My parents rarely took pictures. Film and developing costs were just not in the budget."

"Get the whole batch reprinted if you like," Aly said. She picked up a shot of Marshall taken through the back window of the Cadillac as he got off the school bus when he was in the sixth grade. He wore the usual durable flannel shirt, jeans with darkly patched knees, and what Aly called his Thursday scowl, the look he assumed when he saw the Kingston car in his front yard. "What a proud little boy you were! How you hated being poor!"

"Still would," he said unequivocally, taking the picture from her. He shook his head as if he found it hard to believe that the boy in the picture had ever been he.

"Has being rich made you happy?"

"Not particularly, but I'd rather be unhappy rich than unhappy poor."

"Marshall, did you know Victoria in New York?"

The question took Aly as much by surprise as it did Marshall. He asked cautiously, "Have you ever asked her that question?"

"Yes."

"And?"

"She denied that she saw you."

Marshall frowned. "I can understand that. I was not one of Victoria's greater successes. Nor she mine, for that matter."

"What happened?" Aly asked quietly.

Marshall got up to replace the album on the shelf. His back to her, he answered, "Nothing. That's what happened. You had written Mother that Victoria was working for a modeling agency in New York. I decided to see her." Slipping his hands into his pockets, he turned around, his mood pensive, the dark eyes grave. "I don't know what I had in mind. To be frank, I'd always been ambivalent about Victoria. She was the daughter of a man I hated—I'm not telling you anything there you didn't know, Aly," he said as her brows lifted. He went on, "But like all of us boys, I'd had a yen for her since grade school. She was unaffordable, beyond my reach, so I kept my distance from her." Marshall flashed her a grin. "That Wayne pride, I guess."

Aly nodded. "Go on."

"By the time Victoria arrived in New York, I could afford her. I guess I called her up because I wanted to complete something, then put it behind me."

"Was that the only reason?" Aly asked.

"No." Marshall met her steady gaze. "I hoped to hurt her,

get back at your father through her. I'd always known Victoria wanted me. I was a prize scalp she never got to hang on her belt, so I decided to give her the chance to rectify that situation." He paused. "Am I shooting myself in the foot with this disclosure?"

"No," Aly assured him. "I'd like to know the truth."

"So I began to take her out, and—would you believe?—I liked her. Behind all that scented fluff and self-centeredness was a disappointingly pleasant, decent person. I couldn't have hurt her no matter who her father was."

"So you gave up that idea," Aly said. "Did Victoria…like you?"

"Yes," Marshall answered, understanding her meaning. "If I hurt your sister, it was simply to spare her further hurt. I stopped seeing her when I realized she…cared too much."

In the silence, Marshall went to stare down at the moonlit paddocks and fields. Aly's eyes roved over him admiringly, longingly. Nothing had happened, he had said. Did that mean that his and Victoria's chemistry had simply not ignited or that, quite literally, nothing happened? Did she have the right to ask, given the fact of their own new intimacy? No, she decided. She did not. The question of whether Marshall and Victoria had been together would have to be her own private concern.

Evening had invaded the porch, held off only by the lamps burning on either side of the couch. "Will you be staying the night?" Aly asked.

"No," he said, still staring out at the night. "It's late. You need your sleep for all the work we have to do tomorrow."

Marshall turned too late to see her small smile. Aly accepted the decision without question and escorted him down the breezeway, their arms linked. At the hall tree, he took down his hat. "I'll be out early in the morning. Not here. Green Meadows. See you there."

"I'll look forward to it," she said. "Do you think you might be here through Easter?"

"Easter? When is it?"

"Next Sunday. It's early this year. Green Meadows sponsors an Easter egg hunt in the afternoon for children eleven and under. It's become a traditional event. Everybody comes. You'd have a chance to see a lot of folks you'd miss otherwise."

Next Sunday. The Tuesday after that was the stockholders' meeting. Would Aly have learned about Hattie's shares by then?

"I wouldn't miss it," Marshall said. His gaze questioned her face. "Think you can put up with me that long?"

"You know the answer to that."

"It isn't that I don't want to stay—"

"I understand," she said, smiling and lightly touching his lips with her fingers as if to assure him no more need be said.

Did she? he brooded. Her eyes seemed to hold the understanding of all mysteries, insight into all his secrets and machinations. The lids closed as he lowered his head, shutting off her soul from his view.

Chapter Eleven

Dumbfounded, Aly said, "Victoria, what do you mean, you won't be coming to the Easter egg hunt next Sunday? This is Peter's last year for it. Next year he'll be ineligible. Where will you be?"

"In Duncan. Warren's folks are planning a huge family reunion, and we simply don't have any choice, Aly."

"But—but—can't you drive down after the hunt?"

"No, we can't. It would cut the visit too short. Some of Warren's relatives would be leaving by the time we got there. Besides, we're going camping Thursday through Saturday, then driving to Duncan from wherever we decide to stop overnight."

Aly did not argue. The memory of the last time she had seen her sister was still fresh in her mind and heart, and Aly did not want to risk upsetting her. They had spoken several times on the phone since then, but Victoria had not been out to Cedar Hill, causing Aly to wonder if Victoria feared running into Marshall.

"Does Peter know?"

"Not yet. I'll tell him Thursday morning, and I'd appreciate your not mentioning our plans to the rest of the family. You know how jealous Mother will be that we're spending Easter with the Simses. I'll tell her before we leave."

After she hung up, Aly sat down at her desk in thought, feeling let down. Peter would be heartbroken about missing the hunt. When did the plans for this family reunion in Duncan materialize? Why hadn't Victoria mentioned them earlier? Was the reason because she had wanted to delay as long as possible the disappointing news that her family would be absent at Green Meadows, a day traditionally important to the Kingstons?

Or, Aly wondered, turning over in her mind what Marshall had said about Victoria last night, was it possible that her sister's vanity would not allow her to be around Marshall right now? But that wasn't like Victoria. If her sister minded what she looked like, she would have changed it, and she would never hurt Peter for the sake of her vanity. Aly sighed. She would just have to accept the fact that this year Victoria and her family would be in Duncan for Easter. She had seen for the last time her nephew scampering jackrabbit fashion over a field dotted with brightly colored Easter eggs.

The back door of the office opened abruptly. Marshall, out of breath, poked his head in and announced, "Marigold is about to foal. Willy said you wanted to know."

Aly pushed the button activating the answering service for the phone and hurried with Marshall up the bridle path to the birthing barn. She cast him an amused look. "You're sure...?" Excitement flared in his dark eyes.

"I'll buy you the best steak dinner in Oklahoma if I've missed my guess. She came up to the fence this morning when I went out to check on her and as good as told me she was just about ready to get this show on the road. She headed right into her stall with no problem."

"I'll settle for a riding lesson tonight in case you're wrong."

"You got that anyway. But I'm not wrong."

"The foal's sire is Sampson, you know."

"I know," said Marshall.

In the barn, Aly dispersed the men standing around to other duties and sent Willy to the office to answer the phone, grateful that Marigold would provide yet another experience to convince Marshall he belonged here. She determined that his prognosis was correct. Beads of perspiration dotted Marigold's shoulders and chest, and her tail twitched ceaselessly. As they entered the stall, a stream of white liquid squirted out of a swollen teat.

"She's ready," declared Marshall. "Time to wash her." Aly backed away, letting Marshall take charge and watched him wrap Marigold's tail and cleanse the mare with a mild soap and warm water. Almost as soon as he completed the job, Marigold's sides caved inward, just in front of her hips, a sign that the foal was getting in position to be squeezed through the birth canal. Aly assisted Marshall in helping the mare to lie down, making her as comfortable as her condition would allow.

"Good girl," Marshall kept repeating, stroking the mare's laboring side. Aly stayed unobtrusively in the background, hoping it would not be necessary to remind him that a mare in labor needed her privacy. Unless Marigold needed assistance, she was best left alone during the birth. As if being nudged by her thoughts, Marshall got reluctantly to his feet. "I guess we've done all we can for you, girl. The rest is up to you. We'll be nearby if you need us."

"We can keep an eye on her from the office," Aly said, referring to the waiting room equipped with a closed-circuit television set for monitoring births. "I'll make us some coffee. This may be a long wait."

"I don't think so, but unless I'm needed somewhere else, I'd like to see this through no matter how long it takes."

156

"I believe that can be arranged." Aly smiled.

In the waiting room, snugly outfitted with a sleeping cot and easy chairs, refrigerator and stove for the comfortable waiting out of long hours of labor, Aly made coffee while Marshall stood glued to the monitor screen. One pair of eyes on Marigold was sufficient, she thought, electing to watch him. How very perfect he looked here like this, how very foreign to Wall Street and city crowds and pin-striped suits. He was coming around, she was sure of it. Banking could offer no excitement compared to this. The stockholders' meeting was a week away. If he made no move to part her from her shares before then, she would take that as an indication that he didn't want her stock—he wanted her.

"Look!" he shouted, pointing to the television picture. Aly abandoned the coffeepot and went to his side. Marigold's fetal fluid was gushing out from beneath her tail, a signal that birth would soon follow. Aly checked her watch to begin timing the sequence of events that would determine a normal delivery.

Eventually, after a laborious ten minutes for both Marshall and the mare, a small hoof appeared. Marshall grinned delightedly. "Hot dog!" he said. "So far, so good!"

Finally, as first the tip of a nose, a pair of eyes, ears, then a full head appeared, the little foal slid free of its mother. Marshall gave a whoop of joy. "It's a boy!" he shouted, throwing open the door. "Bring the disinfectant!"

"Yes sir," Aly said with a quiet chuckle.

An hour later, leaving the little colt busy suckling his first meal, Aly and Marshall walked out into the sparkling morning sunshine. "Boy, that was something!" he declared, throwing back his chest and rubbing it in the satisfied manner of a father just told he has a strapping son. "I'd forgotten how good something like that can make you feel. It's been awhile since I've experienced that kind of miracle."

"Or any miracle, I'll bet. New York doesn't seem the climate for them."

"At least it can make you appreciate one when it happens. What do you have lined up for today?"

Aly could hardly keep her pleasure from showing. *Thank you, Marigold.* "The funeral's today, and I'm also finalizing arrangements for Sunday. The ladies' clubs in town are supposed to do all the work, but each year I get roped into more responsibilities. All I'm supposed to provide is the pasture for the egg hunt and a few horses to ride."

"Can I help?"

"You already are." She smiled, wanting to thank him with a good long kiss. "See you here tonight for my first riding lesson?"

"After the men leave. People are beginning to gossip about us, and I don't want to leave you with a spotted reputation—" He called himself a fool the moment he'd said it. Aly looked as if he'd struck her, and of course he knew why.

After several seconds in which she stared at him in dismay, she seemed to draw herself up. "That's noble of you," she said tersely. "By the way, my family will be here Sunday, including Dad. I just thought you ought to know in case you'd like to change your mind about coming. Also, the family will be having dinner together at the house that evening."

Marshall felt as if a cold wind had blown across the sunny morning, chilling the words, the feelings, the moments of a while ago. Hurt lay in the hazel eyes, a stricken sorrow that twisted in his heart like a knife. But he could not retract the statement. He would be leaving. He would have to go once she learned why he'd come. He said quietly, "If I'm still here, I'd like to come. Willy and I can fend for ourselves Sunday evening."

Wordlessly, she left him. Marshall watched her walk down to her office with her shoulders squared against her pain in a way he himself knew only too well.

"I am assuming," Marshall said, "that you know to mount a horse from the left?"

"You would assume correctly, but must you stand so close while I try?" The question was asked curtly, an indication that Aly had not forgotten the morning. She stood with her hand on the saddle pommel of a patient mare that now and then turned her head as if to inquire if Aly were sure she wanted to go through with this.

"Good question, Sure Susan," said Aly, catching the look and turning to interpret for Marshall. They stood so close that her breasts nearly touched his chest. "She wants to know why it's necessary for me to ride her?"

"How else are you to learn to ride?"

"I think the better question that she and I both have in mind is why learn to ride at all? I mean, in my thirty years of living on this earth, I've managed to survive without the joy of cantering across the plains. Why start now?"

"Because otherwise I wouldn't have an excuse to stand near you, touch you, put my arms around you without causing talk." Marshall reached to grip the pommel with one hand and the rear of the saddle with the other, enclosing her in an embrace made more provocative because he did not touch her. "Why didn't you tell me the trainers would be working late tonight?"

Feeling her senses beginning to respond in spite of the severe lecture she'd given herself this morning, Aly nonetheless met his gaze imperturbably. In the next field over, several trainers were putting a number of Thoroughbreds through their paces. "The owners of those animals are picking them up sooner than expected," Aly answered, wishing she could slip her arms up around his neck and draw him down to her. How heavenly to feel herself enfolded and borne away to the same sensual oblivion where he had taken her once before. But she would never be taken there again, she knew that now. What a fool she had been to think there were only two courses of action open to Marshall.

She saw another possibility: he could string her along until she was sick with love for him. Then, perhaps playing on the antipathy he guessed still existed between her and her father, casually let out the truth about his scheme to take over the bank. The final step had been to buy Hattie's stock, but that failing, he guessed his thirteen-year venture had come to nought, and he'd be heading back up to New York. Unless, of course, she could see her way clear to let him have *her* shares. Then he could take over the bank and live in Claiborne for the rest of his life. How would she like that?

At which point she hoped she still had the wherewithal to give Marshall Wayne succinct instructions about what he could do both with his suggestion and the rest of his life.

She was such a black-and-white, all-or-nothing kind of person. A third possibility had not occurred to her—that Marshall might care too much for her to divest her of her shares but not enough to stay. What an idiot she had been to think her house and the breeding farm, a few snapshots from the past and a foal's birth—that *she*—could lure him back to Claiborne.

"Kindly back away before we give those trainers something to talk about tomorrow," Aly ordered crisply.

Marshall dropped his arms. Something she could not decipher flashed in his eyes. "I'll hold the reins while you mount," he said. When she had slung herself onto the saddle, he handed them to her. "We'll ride in that direction," he instructed, pointing toward two bluffs in the distance.

Aly already knew how to sit a horse and the rudiments of rein direction. Because she lacked the beginner's fear of horses, soon she and Marshall, astride Sampson, were riding at a prudent speed toward the bluffs. The twilight lingered, a moon rose to give them further light, and the strain between them settled into an accepting silence as they rode through meadows carpeted in wildflowers.

The bluffs, almost twin in size, gave the impression that eons ago some tremendous force had bowled across the plains and severed them in two. The fissure between them created a narrow valley that Aly wanted Marshall to see. In late spring it offered a scenic delight so unusual that a trip to the bluffs on horseback had become one of the major activities at Green Meadows on Easter Sunday.

"My God," breathed Marshall as they reined in at the mouth of the valley. "What are they?"

"Love-Lies-Bleeding is the common name," Aly answered, naming the mass of red wildflowers whose spiked clusters were just beginning to form. Later on the blooms would droop in long tassels like ropes of chenille, creating a spectacular sight. They filled the valley floor from one end to the other as if their seeds had been accidentally jostled from a giant hand countless springs ago. Nowhere else in Oklahoma were they known to bloom and flourish. "I discovered this valley when I was trying to decide how much land I wanted to buy. I took a jeep out on a surveying mission and came upon this sight in June six years ago."

Marshall turned in the saddle to look back over the distance they had come. "You own all this land?"

Aly nodded. "If my plans for Green Meadows materialize, I'll need every acre. Shall we go wading?" She indicated the sea of red flowers undulating in the late evening breeze.

Marshall urged Sampson forward. "Love-Lies-Bleeding. That's an unusual name. Rather sorrowful. Where does it come from?"

"I don't know, but it seems appropriate. These flowers never seem to wither; they thrive with very little care in dry heat and poor soil and can be transplanted easily." She gave him a quick, unforgiving smile. "Much like the cultural properties of love."

"Is that so?" Marshall answered quietly.

"Much like mine, anyway," Aly said flatly, and fell silent. They did not speak again until they had traversed the valley. Side by side they rode through the moving sea of tasseling blooms, watched over by a merry, fat-cheeked moon hanging above the crevice directly before them. At the other end, when they had reined in, Marshall leaned over and laid his hand over hers on the pommel.

"I knew this would happen, Aly," he said gently, "and I'm sorry. It wouldn't work between us, you know, no matter what you might think now."

Unable to look at him, her throat tight, Aly said obstinately, "Yes, it would. We belong together, Marshall Wayne. We always have."

"You think so now, Aly—"

"I've thought so all my life!" she cried, waving her hand to indicate the acres over which they'd just traveled. "You could share all of this with me. What is New York compared to this? What can there be about banking or—or commodities that is half as exciting as seeing that colt born this morning?" Tears glimmered in her eyes. Her voice broke as she said, "Who would ever love you as much as I?"

"Honey—" Marshall had not taken his hand away. "That's not the point."

The statement made her look directly at him. She was glad

that in the growing darkness he had not seen the tears she had blinked away. "No, it isn't, is it?" she said, her voice hard. She was a bigger fool than she'd thought. Marshall had not been falling in love with her. "You know," she said, "you are a most fortunate man to have been spared the suffering you've caused so many women, deliberate or not. Your love will never lie bleeding."

Marshall took his hand away. "Oh, I don't know," he said. "Maybe we'd better start back now."

"And just how," she snapped, her heart breaking, "do I get Sure Susan to understand that?"

Darkness fell as they neared the barn, though the moon still smiled. "I'll put the horses away," Marshall said. He looked at her in concern. "May I take you out to supper somewhere?"

"No thank you," Aly said, her chin raised, her voice remote. "I have work to do at the office. Thanks for the ride, Marshall. I'll never forget it."

She left him to walk back down to her office alone, aware from his expression that he had understood the barbed irony of her last remark. *That was unfair*, she reprimanded herself as she hurried along the lamplit bridle path. *Marshall didn't take you on any ride you didn't hop on willingly. You ought to be thankful he put the brakes on when he did. Otherwise you'd be in worse shape when he leaves than you are already.*

But there were tears in her eyes when she answered the phone that rang as she unlocked the door to her office. It was her father, calling to inform her of two displeasures. "Aly, is Marshall working out at Green Meadows?"

"He's filling in for Joe until next Sunday."

"Have you taken leave of your senses? You know how vulnerable you've always been to Marshall!"

"And you know how invulnerable Marshall has always been to me."

"Alyson, a man doesn't have to *admire* a woman to divest her of *everything*!"

"Anything else, Dad?"

"Yes," Lorne snapped. "The proxies are continuing to come in negative."

"You don't have anything to worry about, Dad. Take my word for it. Good night."

Aly was still holding the phone when Marshall came in the back door. "Trouble?" he asked.

"That was my father," she explained.

Marshall grew rigid. "What did he say to upset you so?"

She smiled at him faintly. "Nothing that I didn't know already."

"Aly—" Marshall went to her, taking her by the shoulders. He studied her closely for the signs he expected, but her face seemed drawn only from the emotional travails of the day. "Let me help if I can."

"There is nothing you can do. Dad is just Dad. Not to worry," she said, patting his hand and moving away from him.

"No matter what our differences," he said to her back, "I'm not leaving until Joe comes back. You need all the help you can get out here."

She faced him. "I'm glad," she said simply. "Now if you'll excuse me, Marshall, I have work to do."

Preparations for Easter Sunday kept Aly busy during the remainder of the week. She saw Marshall infrequently but strained for a glimpse of him every time she passed an office window or walked along the bridle paths. The pasture next to her house was mowed, the terrain checked for holes that might hide rattlesnakes and other dangers for children searching for Easter eggs in the grass. Aly met with the leaders of womens' groups that annually set up and manned booths selling refreshments, baked goods, and seedlings for spring gardens. The far corner of the pasture was reserved for a catering firm that would be serving a noonday meal of barbecued beef and ham and all the trimmings for a price, which would be shared with local charity organizations. By Saturday afternoon, boxes containing hundreds of brightly colored eggs lined the breezeway.

That afternoon Aly happened to be on the back porch when she spotted Marshall in a field adjoining the one cleared for the hunt. He had brought out two Thoroughbreds in a horse trailer to turn loose for grazing. "Marshall!" she called to him from the back door, waving to catch his attention. He did not see her, and the distance was too great for her to be heard. She went down the steps through the cedars to the edge of the cleared field, afraid that he would be pulling out in the trailer before she got there.

It had been a terribly depressing day. Tomorrow completed Marshall's week. How soon afterward would he leave? It would have been better if Peter had been around, helping her to sort the eggs, getting more and more excited as Sunday drew nearer. But, come to think of it, maybe he wouldn't have been so excited this year. He was growing up. Already his face was maturing, slimming into the devastatingly spare features she thought so handsome in a man.

"Marshall!" she called again with an ache in her throat. *Speaking of handsome!* He had turned her way, and her heart caught at the swift smile that lit his face when he saw her. How tall he was, how virile and lean in his jeans and western shirt. How could she live when he had gone?

Cupping her hands around her mouth, she called to him, "Would you like to come up to the house for a cup of coffee?"

He waved in response. "Be right there!" he hollered back, and she thought he looked delighted.

Aly ran back to the house, her heart lighter. Had it only been ten days since she saw Marshall in the airport in Dallas? It seemed both a lifetime and, at the same time, only a few precious seconds, as evaporative as raindrops in her hand. But she would make the most of the days left, holding them fast as long as she could.

She had the coffee on by the time he came up the back steps. "Good afternoon," she hailed him cheerfully, taking his hat. "As your dad used to say, 'Come in and take a load off your feet.'"

Marshall laughed. "He did say that, didn't he? How have you been, Aly?"

All week he had expected to look up from his chores to find her storming up the bridle path with blood in her eyes. But still she didn't know, he could tell from her happy smile at seeing him, at his being here. God, how he wished he could stay!

"Busy," she answered, gesturing toward the breezeway. "I don't know how we would have managed this week without you, Marshall."

Marshall glanced toward the breezeway. "What's out there?"

"See for yourself."

Marshall walked to the door of the long hall. "Good Lord!" he exclaimed at the sight of the eggs. "You have been busy. Did you do all of these yourself?"

"Can't take credit for a single one. I've just been collecting them. I have my share already boiled and ready to dye tonight. Want to help?"

Marshall turned to her with a doubtful look. "Sure it's all right?"

"Marshall," she said on a deep, frank sigh, "if you say no, I think I just may kill myself."

"Can't have that." He grinned. "I'll pick up supper when I go to the motel to change."

When Marshall arrived later with their dinner—a box of commercially prepared chicken, slaw, and fresh tomatoes and ears of corn bought at a roadside stand—Aly had changed into a pink terrycloth jumpsuit. It hugged her slim figure becomingly and brought out the healthy color of her cheeks. Her hair had been brushed into a shining topknot from which a few tendrils had escaped at the nape of her neck. A light application of makeup enhanced her eyes and mouth.

"You look refreshed," said Marshall, handing her his purchases. Actually, she looked downright seductive in a squeaky-clean kind of way. "That shower did wonders for you."

"It was a bath," she said.

"Yes," he said, drawing closer. "You smell like bubble bath."

Aly cleared her throat, wondering if he could hear the hammerblows of her heart. "Thanks for the meal," she said, the packages between them. "I've been too busy even to think about eating. You want to dye first and then eat, or eat first and then dye?" She rounded her eyes at him over the sacks, the joy of being with him making them bright.

Marshall considered a moment. "Let's have a drink first and dip while we sip. Then we'll sup."

"Cute." Aly laughed, leading him down the breezeway. "Real cute."

Two dozen brilliantly dyed eggs later, they sat side by side on the porch couch with their feet propped on the coffee table and admired their handiwork. "They're masterpieces," proclaimed Marshall proudly. He was on a third Scotch and water, and Aly couldn't determine if the pleasure of her company or the liquor was responsible for his high spirits. She didn't care. She intended to enjoy every minute as it came.

"You'll come tomorrow?" she asked.

"Wouldn't miss it. Your whole family will be coming, you say?"

"Victoria and her family won't be. They'll be at a family reunion in Duncan."

"Too bad," he said. "I'd have liked to have seen her again, met her husband and son."

Which means, Aly thought, her joy suddenly gone, that tomorrow would be his only opportunity to do so. He'd be leaving before he saw Victoria again.

By evening's end, a sadness had descended between them. "Good night, beautiful lady," Marshall whispered at the oval-glassed door. He touched a tendril of hair curling softly next to one ear. "Remember always, Aly, that it wasn't you." He kissed her quickly and was gone.

Dawn had just broken the next morning when Aly and her group of organizers assembled to begin hiding the eggs. Several husbands as well as Willy had been commanded to erect booths and canopies and unload pickups. The group had just gathered around a table Aly had set up with coffee and doughnuts when a white Lincoln turned up the drive of Cedar Hill.

"Lor', if it ain't Marshall, Punkin," said Willy. "I didn't think he planned to help."

At the sight of the handsome head behind the wheel, Aly felt her own dawn break inside her. "Neither did I," she said and went to meet him.

Marshall assisted the men first, but after a while he came to take eggs from Aly's box and camouflage them with sand and grass near where she hid hers. No words passed between them. Aly watched the deft, slender hands, conscious of the simple specialness of their shared labor on this Easter morning as the sunrise broke over them.

When they had finished the far corner of the field, Aly picked up the empty box. "All through," she said regretfully.

"Not quite."

She was suddenly in his arms in the shadow of the caterer's shed. For the second it took his head to descend, Aly glimpsed a look that she would have sold her soul to understand. Afterward she searched his face. "Seems to me that was rather desperate, Marshall Wayne. Are you by any chance trying to make up your mind about something?"

"No," he said brusquely. "Let's get back to the others."

"Well, Marshall, and to what do we owe the pleasure of your unexpected return to Claiborne?" asked Lorne Senior affably. Aly knew that the expansive manner was being assumed to imply there was nothing to worry him on this lovely Easter Sunday. He regarded Marshall as if he were a mere speck of dust easily brushed off his impeccable dark blue suit.

The Kingston family, as in all years past, had been the last to arrive. Like royalty, they descended from their new Cadillac—black, as in all years, but bought on the installment plan this time—and strolled, smiles fixed, toward their waiting subjects.

Marshall returned the broad smile, his eyes cold. "I was curious to see if anything had changed."

"That so?" said Lorne, lifting lordly brows. "And have you found anything changed?"

"Cedar Hill for the better since the last time I saw it. And of course Aly. Otherwise, I've found everything and everyone very much the same."

"You must find that gratifying."

"I do. Believe me."

For a finite second the gray eyes looked uncertain. Lorne turned to his son. "You remember Lorne Junior."

Lorne Junior, his waist and neck beginning to show the ease of his nine-to-five position at the bank and his six-to-ten position at home, wrung Marshall's hand congenially. "Guess you'll be leaving soon, huh? Can't imagine there's anything here now for a big-city feller such as yourself."

"Oh, I don't know..."

Aly, listening to this well-gloved sparring with suspended heartbeat, sensed her father stiffen as Marshall looked her way.

A record crowd enjoyed the finest spring day for the Easter event in its six-year history. So glorious was the sunshine, so clear the sky and delicate the breeze, that when Willy, who happened to be in the house when the phone rang, came limping out at top speed to report a tornado on the way, those who heard him at first disregarded his babble as a sick joke. But no sooner had the report begun its rounds than a change occurred in the atmosphere. The light little breeze, like a kitten suddenly turned tiger, began to nip through thin Easter dresses and lightweight suits. Leaden gray skies overtook the sunshine. A vigilant hush fell over the crowd except for the squeals and laughter of children playing in the field.

In alarm, Aly looked around for Marshall who materialized beside her as if out of her thoughts. He took her arm just as someone pointed and cried, "Oh, my God! Look what's coming!"

Chapter Twelve

Get under the van!" Marshall shouted above the hysterical din of screams and shouts, the freight-train roar that suddenly filled the once-still afternoon. He scooped up two children whose faces still registered the shock of seeing their Easter baskets snatched from their hands by the dusty winds preceding the black funnel twisting across the plains.

Aly obeyed, managing, with Marshall and his charges right behind her, to herd another small child under the low frame of the Winnebago just before the fury hit. Ear-deafening and unearthly in its power, it slammed like an enraged beast into the vehicle, rocking it back and forth over the helpless victims pressed into the earth below. The ground exploded around them, stunning and choking, pelting arms and legs with burning rubber. Aly could only surmise that the van must have been picked up and set back down with such force that all six tires had blown at once.

Later they learned the insanity lasted only five minutes. To Aly it seemed more like a lifetime in hell. She would remember always, more profoundly than the moment she realized they had survived the ordeal, the sound of Marshall's voice in her ear when the calm had come. "Aly? Aly? Say something to me, honey!"

"I'm all right, Marshall," she assured him, spitting out dust and shifting away from the protection of his body to release three squirming little figures who wriggled out from under the Winnebago in crying search of their parents.

Marshall squinted at her through sand-coated lashes. The side of his mouth quirked. "I'll say one thing. When Alyson Kingston throws a party, she throws a party."

Overcome with inexpressible gratitude, Aly answered by wordlessly laying a grimy hand against his gritty cheek. Marshall's hand closed over it. Then they heard the first stirrings and cries of the survivors. "Not everybody seems to have had a good time," she said. "Let's go see what that gatecrasher did."

They crawled out from under the wrecked camper to a spectacle not quite resembling the atomic aftermath Aly had expected. Vehicles lay overturned and the debris of canopies and sheds littered the fields. A whole side of beef, dripping barbeque sauce, had caught in the sagging fence. She took a deep breath and looked toward the house. Miracle of miracles, it was still there. The top of one chimney had been sliced off, part of the roof had lost some shingles, and the cedar trees in front lay in a straight, serried file as if felled by one gigantic ax stroke at their base. But the house still stood.

Searching for her family among the dazed and recovering people who had not made the safety of the house and storm shelter but had hidden under cars and trucks, Aly was amazed that no one had suffered more serious injury. The cries seemed to be coming more from fright and relief than pain.

"I think we just got a nip of the damned thing," opined a weather-wise farmer to Aly, looking off toward the direction the tornado must have taken. "I think it's headed straight for Claiborne."

Others agreed and while Marshall and Willy headed for the

barns to check on the horses, Aly went to the house to seek her family, grateful that Peter and his parents were in Duncan.

Her father met her at the door of her house, impeccable and calm, but startlingly aged. "Aly!" He said her name with such relief that for one of the few times in her life, she went to him and put her arms around him. She felt him tremble as he embraced her.

"It's all right, Dad. I'm okay. How's Mother?"

"Shaken up, of course, but otherwise all right. She's lying down. We were in the house when it hit. On occasions like these, people are inclined to get sticky fingers. We thought our presence might be an effective deterrent."

"Thank you, Dad. I noticed a couple of windows broken in your car, but it should get you and Mother home. That is…"

Lorne looked at her sharply. "That is what?" he said.

"Well, the tornado seems headed for Claiborne. We must have just gotten a sideswipe—"

"Good God!" exclaimed Lorne.

"Let's go check the weather news. That is, if the electricity is still on."

"It was last time I checked. Also the phone is still working." Her father pulled out a gold pocket watch. "I think, however, I'll go collect your mother and we'll be on our way. I'm curious to see the damage, which should have been done by now." He turned back to her as they started inside. "By the way, Aly, if I don't see you before Tuesday morning—"

"Oh, Dad," Aly spoke in disappointment. "You can't have the stockholders' meeting on your mind at a time like this?"

Ignoring the question, Lorne said, "Most of the proxies have arrived, and as I suspected, they have voted against retaining the present board. That look young Marshall gave you a while ago—you know the one I mean. Has it any significance?"

"None whatsoever. He was just needling you."

"And I need have no fear that you will do something foolish?"

"Not in the least."

"Good," he said with satisfaction. "I have always relied on your word, Aly, for the simple reason you've never broken it."

Only part of Claiborne found itself in the path of the storm. The wrath of the tornado veered away from most schools, churches, and businesses, bypassing the wealthiest and poorest residential sections to concentrate almost solely on the middle-class neighborhoods. Victoria's house was in one of these. The Kingston State Bank remained unscathed.

"Never mind, darling," said her mother the next morning as the Kingston women gathered to help Victoria sort through the mess for salvageable items, "you can live with us until a new house is built. This time you'll build in our neighborhood."

Which will insure protection from further tornadoes, Aly flashed to Victoria, who smiled wanly in understanding, her eyes still glazed from the shock of finding her home demolished. "Where do you want us to start?" Aly asked.

"You start over there," said Victoria, pointing to a space that had once been the library. "You'll know what's important among Warren's papers to try to salvage. The rest of us will just look for anything keepable."

Due to the rain that had fallen in the wake of the tornado, everything was sodden. The women had been sorting for an hour with very little to show for their labor when Aly came across a heavy-duty, letter-sized portfolio half-buried in the mud. Aly untied the string and drew out a number of documents. One was Victoria's marriage license. Though damp, the signature of the justice of the peace and the typed information stating date and place of the marriage remained decipherable.

Aly puzzled over the date. It declared that Victoria married a month later than the anniversary she and Warren celebrated each year. There must have been a mistake.

On the verge of bringing it to Victoria's attention, Aly lifted her head and looked across what was left of the hall at her sister sorting through the remnants of a record collection. Then something—a conviction that went through her with a decimating certainty—made her cry out. Victoria glanced over at her, the blue eyes wide with alarm. "Aly? What's the matter?"

"Nothing really," Aly said, her vision hazy. "I—had a pain across my chest, that's all."

Victoria got up, her expression worried. "What kind of pain?"

"Pleurisy, I guess." She smiled fleetingly. "Grandmother used to have it."

"You've never complained of it before."

"I was in the rain so much yesterday, trying to round up the horses." Aly rubbed the area above her left breast. "I probably caught a cold or something..."

"Let me get Mother—"

"No—no, Victoria." Aly looked over at their mother a good distance away. She was intent on the task of sorting through her grandson's clothes. "Here," she said, pushing the documents back into the folder. She thrust it at her sister. "These seem relatively undamaged. I'd better go home. Don't say anything to Mother."

"Aly, your eyes look like a wasteland. Are you sure you're all right? Why don't I come with you?"

"No, I'm fine, really, Victoria. Say hello to your men for me." She summoned a smile and called good-bye to her mother and sister-in-law, who was working a number of rooms over. Forc-

175

ing her legs to her car, she saw that Victoria still gazed after her as she drove off, the mud-covered portfolio in her hand.

In the car, Aly moaned her grief aloud, gripping the steering wheel. She sped toward Cedar Hill, where she had always taken her griefs. *Elizabeth*, she sobbed inwardly. *Elizabeth!*

She left her car in front and used the handrail to help her up the porch steps. Once inside she collapsed on the chair by the refectory table. She sat there, staring at the aquarium whose denizen-life had begun to return to normal after the disruption of the storm.

She had always assumed that Victoria had eloped with Warren on the rebound after an ego-shattering affair in New York. And this only after the facts indisputably cleared Victoria from the suspicion that she was pregnant when she married. Today's evidence proved otherwise. Peter was one month on the way when his mother stood before that justice of the peace.

Now Victoria's odd reaction to Marshall, her denial that she had seen him in New York were explained. No wonder she had not introduced Peter to him. No wonder she had taken her family somewhere else for Easter. She had wanted to keep Peter away from his father. Marshall was Peter's father.

Aly picked up her most recent picture of Peter from the table. She should have suspected the truth earlier. Already father and son were beginning to look alike. Those dark brown eyes and lean good looks they had in common. How long before Peter's hair turned darker, increasing their resemblance? Elizabeth had said that Marshall had been born with blond hair. The irony was that Marshall did not suspect the truth either. He had no idea that Victoria had been pregnant with his child when she left New York.

Now what? Victoria was worried sick that Marshall might discover the truth. No doubt right now she was blessing the tornado that justified leaving Peter in Duncan for a few days. Marshall would be gone by the time she collected him again. He most likely would never come back now that he had lost the bid to take over the bank.

The phone rang beside her, all but jerking her out of her skin. She answered it reluctantly, thinking Victoria was calling to check on her welfare. But Joe was on the other end. "Aly?" he said.

The silky way he said it sent a crawly feeling down her backbone. "Yes, Joe?"

"In sorting through Aunt Hattie's desk, I came across the last annual report of the Kingston State Bank. Found it mighty interesting reading after I had a friend of mine who knows about such things explain it to me."

"That so, Joe?" Aly struggled to keep her voice conversational.

"Uh-huh. He told me some things that you should have told me, Aly. He told me that you don't have to own the majority of stock to control it. I reckon Marshall came to town in control of enough shares to take care of your dad for good once he bought Aunt Hattie's stock. But then I imagine you figured that out for yourself the night I was out there."

Sitting very still, Aly did not reply. Joe continued. "So I figure that since I'm not selling my shares, Marshall is out there at Green Meadows sniffing after yours, a fact you also know. Would I be right about that, Aly?"

After a brief pause, Aly replied, "Go on."

"Well, right now I'm just guessing, but knowing you, I figure that you're giving that lad enough rope either to reel him in or to hang himself. Which is it?"

"Joe, that has to be my business."

"I see. Well, Miss Kingston, I don't mind sharing my business with you, not at all. Because I still owe you for Benjy, I'm gonna wait until this all-fired important stockholders' meeting for this little game of yours to play itself out. Then I'm selling my shares Wednesday morning, the minute Judge Peabody finishes the probate hearing and releases Aunt Hattie's assets to me. Otherwise, I end up with nothing, don't you see—no money and no girl."

Aly froze. "Who—who—do you plan to sell them to?"

"Why Marshall, of course. That way I have the satisfaction of doing what Aunt Hattie would have wanted."

"Joe, listen!" Aly gripped the receiver. Good Lord, if Joe sold them to Marshall, he would stay in Claiborne. As majority stockholder, he would be able to accomplish on Wednesday what he would not be able to do tomorrow. Even if she informed her father now of Joe's intent, he would not have enough time to block the takeover. "Sell the stock to me," she pleaded. "I'll pay you anything you ask—"

"Too late, Miss Kingston," Joe sneered. "You should have made me that offer before you threatened me on account of Marshall. Now you're going to find that not only did you lose a man you never had, but you've just lost the best stable manager in Oklahoma. The only thing you're getting from me is the promise that I won't say anything to Marshall until Wednesday. You can send me the wages I got coming. So long, Miss Kingston." He hung up.

Aly sat in stunned anguish. It would only be a matter of time before Peter matured into a recognizable semblance of his real father. What would Marshall do when he perceived the likeness? Would he identify himself to Peter? Would he fight for him? A custody battle would cause more scandal and damage, ruin the Kingstons more thoroughly than taking over a hundred of their banks.

Aly's head jerked up. Her body stiffened as an idea began to form. She would make a trade. She would trade her shares for Peter... She got up, paced in thought for a few minutes. No one need ever know her real reason for giving Marshall the stock that would allow him to take over the Kingston State Bank. Everyone would think that she was so besotted over him—hadn't she always been?—that he'd been able to finagle her into selling out her family to him. But with acceptance of her stock would go a condition. Marshall would have to promise that he would leave Claiborne and never return. He could run the bank from a distance. He could sell it. He could appoint a chairman and a president. She didn't care what arrangments he made as long as they did not include living in Claiborne where someday he would discover Victoria's secret.

She sat down again, confused and sorrowful. Was she doing the right thing? Did she have the right to keep Marshall from knowing his child? Did she have the right to do this to her father and Lorne Junior? Her family would never forgive her. They would call her a traitor and a fool, a woman who not only lost her family and the bank, but lost the man for whom she had sacrificed them. But what else could she do? A little boy's happiness was at stake, his future, his life. None of their lives, their happiness were more important than his. Her father, Victoria, Marshall—they all had themselves to thank for the decision she was forced to make. Peter shouldn't be made to suffer for the mistakes that would drive a wedge between himself and the man he thought his father. He shouldn't have to bear the ridicule and scandal that would be sure to follow. He might never recover from such a trauma.

Slowly, Aly pulled out a drawer in the refectory table. She took out paper and pen. "Dear Marshall..." she began.

*　　*　　*

The Claiborne Public Library, its plain white stucco frame embellished by a decade's growth of climbing ivy and banks of bright yellow forsythia, had been spared so much as the disturbance of a leaf by the tornado. The building reposed on a lush lawn at the end of the residential street where her parents lived, and Aly hoped that her car would escape notice from someone in the house.

Miss Trudy Templeton, the aged librarian with whom Aly had been friends since she was old enough to read, greeted her visitor warmly. "Alyson, dear, I was so happy to hear that Green Meadows was spared. What a shame if that beautiful house had been destroyed and those lovely horses left homeless."

"We were very fortunate, as were you, it seems," said Aly, looking around at her childhood sanctuary. "I have a favor to ask you, Miss Trudy. I want you to witness and notarize something. You've still got your seal, haven't you?"

"Oh, dear me, yes. Wouldn't give it up for the world. How else would I be privy to half the secrets of Claiborne? Not that I ever tell them, mind you," she twinkled conspiratorially.

A few minutes later, Miss Trudy was affixing her seal to a letter of proxy giving Marshall the right to vote her shares in the coming stockholders' meeting. The librarian glanced over it, then at Aly. "Lordy sakes, but this news would rival the tornado *were I to make it known*." She emphasized the last heavily. "Are you sure you want to go through with this?"

Aly nodded, remembering how Trudy Templeton had disapproved the foreclosure of Cedar Hill. "By tomorrow at lunch everybody will know its contents anyway, so after that you might as well go ahead and add your earful."

What's this? Marshall asked himself, thinking he knew as he tore open the flap of an envelope bearing the return address of Cedar

Hill. Before going to his motel room he had checked at the desk to see if Aly might have left him a note explaining her disappearance. They had not been worried about her out at Green Meadows until Victoria had appeared in the doorway of one of the barns exclaiming that she'd not been able to find Aly anywhere. Then they'd all been frantic until Aly called Willy to say that she was in Oklahoma City.

"Where is she staying in Oklahoma City?" Victoria had demanded when Marshall called her after speaking with Willy.

"I don't know, Victoria. She wouldn't say."

"When will she be back?"

"She didn't say that either."

"Marshall Wayne, you're the cause of all this!" The phone had gone down with a bang, and Marshall had felt a claw of fear rake his spine.

Now he drew out two sheets of paper. His eyes would not let him believe the first. It was a signed, witnessed, and notarized letter of proxy giving him the right to vote Aly's shares in the stockholders' meeting tomorrow. The note stated that the shares would be reissued in his name at one o'clock on one condition. The condition was explained.

Fatigue gone, every corpuscle alert to the significance of the terse wording, Marshall crumpled the note in his hand. So now she knew. She knew everything. And she had given him the means to destroy Lorne Kingston.

At nine o'clock the next morning while Marshall, she assumed, was dressing for the stockholders' meeting, Aly had finished a third cup of coffee in the restaurant of the motel where she had spent a sleepless night. No use dallying any longer, she said to herself. She had to get back and face all the music. *Where did the negative implication of that cliché come from*, she wondered irrelevantly. *Face the music.* She loved music. After today there would be little enough of it in her life.

Aly summoned the waitress for her bill. At the door, hand on its crossbar, she paused a moment, reflecting that from this exit on, her life would never be the same.

At five minutes until ten, Marshall Wayne strolled into the conference room of the Kingston State Bank where the rest of the stockholders had already assembled and were helping themselves to doughnuts and coffee. Marshall nodded pleasantly as he approached the refreshment table, seemingly unaware of the gradual silence falling at his entrance. He had never looked more urbane. Faultlessly attired in a gray suit and crisp blue shirt, silk tie and highly polished shoes, he appeared the ultimate New York banker.

"Good morning," he said congenially as Lorne Senior, complacency sliding from his face like gray paint down smoothly weathered wood, cut through the group to confront him.

"What are you doing here? You're not a stockholder."

"Today I am." Marshall handed the banker Aly's proxy letter.

Lorne read the contents, then gaped at him in speechless incredulity for a full minute while Marshall casually munched a doughnut. "She—she—can't do this!" Lorne gasped at last. "She can't do this…"

Oh, Lord, not now, Aly lamented silently, seeing Victoria's blue station wagon parked in the drive. Of all people she could do without seeing at the moment, it was Victoria. Immediately, she regretted the thought. After this morning, her sister might never set foot in her house again.

"Where have you been?" Victoria demanded, meeting Aly at

the door. "We've all been worried sick about you. Why didn't you let us know where you were going?"

"I'm sorry to have worried you," Aly said. "I—I just wanted to be alone for a while. It must have been a delayed reaction to the shock of the tornado, seeing your house and so many others destroyed—"

"Phooey! It wasn't that, and you know it. Nothing in this world has ever made you turn tail and run, Aly Kingston, nothing! Not even dear old Dad!" She yanked open her purse and pulled out the marriage license. "It was this, wasn't it, that made you leave so suddenly yesterday."

Aly wanted to deny it, but she hadn't the strength. She nodded slowly.

"Well, let's go in here and talk about it," Victoria said in a softer tone and took Aly's arm. "To tell you the truth, I'm relieved that you know, although I am a little surprised at your reaction. You've always been so broadminded and accepting. I'd have predicted that you'd simply shrug and say so what." She led the way into the front parlor.

Aly stared after her. Victoria's brain power had not improved since her marriage, but her sensibilities had. Surely she had not missed all these years how much she cared for Marshall.

"Now let's just sit down and have a woman-to-woman talk," Victoria suggested, patting the sofa. "I want to tell you about Peter's father."

Reluctantly, Aly sat down beside her. "If you don't mind, Victoria, I'd really rather not know about Peter's father—"

"Well, I want you to know!" Victoria declared in a voice that echoed her old self. "I don't want you thinking badly of me."

"I don't think badly of you, Victoria."

"Well, you're acting like it," she said, and added, "Aly, Peter will never know, so you don't have to worry about that."

Aly swallowed. "I hope you're right."

"I lied to you about not knowing Marshall in New York."

"Yes, I know. He told me," Aly whispered.

Victoria did not seem to notice the pain in her sister's eyes. Settling herself, she began her narrative. "He called me up out of the blue and asked me out. You can imagine how surprised I was. Here I thought he hated every one of us Kingstons after what Dad did to Cedar Hill. I'd always had as mad a crush on him as you did, I think. So I jumped at the chance to go out with him. I was rather glad to be burying the hatchet, at least between us. Dad could look after himself, as I saw it. Anyway, we went out a few times, and I..." Victoria flushed and looked away. "Well, you know how irresistible Marshall is."

"Yes," Aly said softly.

"So I—I fell for him, only he didn't fall for me. He was nice about it and all, nicer than he had to be, actually, but the plain truth was, he dumped me."

"Victoria, you don't have to say anything more." Aly laid a restraining hand on her sister's arm."

"Yes, I do, Aly, or you won't understand everything fully."

"All right, Victoria."

"So after Marshall left my life, I went a little crazy, I think. Nobody had ever thrown me over before, and it was a strange and frightening feeling. There I was alone in New York and blue. I started eating. I gained weight. I began to lose my confidence. And that's when I met—" She stopped, looked at Aly covertly. "No names. I'm not going to tell you his name. But he was tall and dark-eyed and handsome as the dickens, and I was so in need of a man to bandage my ego."

Aly withdrew her hand carefully, so as not to give away the surprise and relief beginning to course through her. Light

glimmered through the darkness of her despair. "This man...
looked like Marshall somewhat?" she suggested.

Victoria considered. "Well, a little, I guess. Both have the
same kind of dark eyes and those long, lean frames that are so
sexy. I had to prove to myself that just because Marshall didn't
want me in *that way* didn't mean another ultraattractive man
wouldn't."

"I understand, Victoria," Aly said, her profound relief giving
way to the horrifying realization of what she had done. The
rest of the story came to her ears as a garble. Her mind had
jumped to the scene of Marshall in the conference room voting
her proxy against the board...

"...And Marshall's sudden appearance brought back everything, panicked me so," Victoria was explaining when Aly returned to her. "He—he—was so close to my secret, like a threat
to it. He saw me one night with—with the man I was seeing.
We were in a restaurant and I had to introduce them. I was
afraid that somehow Marshall might guess...Peter looks so like
his father. And then when you said what you did about my marrying Warren on the rebound—well, Aly, you can imagine how
I felt!"

"Yes, I can imagine." Aly swallowed.

"I lied about Marshall because I thought that might protect
my secret. If I hadn't known Marshall in New York, how could
he have met Peter's father, you see."

"I see," said Aly.

"But if I hadn't known...that man in New York," Victoria
caught herself, "I wouldn't have had Peter. And I might not
have married Warren. And I might have stayed that stuck-up
pain-in-the-you-know-what." Victoria's laughter bubbled out
as she hugged her sister. "And you and I might not have become
such good friends, dear sister of mine." She looked at Aly con-

tritely, her mouth pursed in pretty appeal. "I'm sorry I lied to you, and I'm sorry we had to miss your Easter party. Forgiven?"

"Forgiven and the rest forgotten," Aly said. A cold inertia had taken control of her limbs. "It's just as well you were in Duncan Sunday," she managed to add.

"Well, I'm going to get out of here and let you get some rest. You look tired, Alyson. Oops, there's your phone. Want me to get it?"

"Uh, no," said Aly quickly, getting to her feet. "I'll get it, Victoria. Thanks." It was probably their father, and she wanted to spare Victoria the news of her betrayal as long as she could—to remember the moment between them untarnished.

"Toodle then," said Victoria, going to the door. "I'm going to Duncan in the morning to pick up Peter. Okay if he stays with you tomorrow night? He's dying to."

Aly smiled faintly. "I'll be here."

Moving slowly, Aly reached the phone on its fifth ring. She lifted the receiver. "Alyson?"

Her heart clutched. "Yes, Dad?"

"My dear, you are indeed your father's daughter."

"Yes, I come by certain of my...attributes honestly." Pain shot across her chest. Her father's anger, over its first explosive phase, had settled into the smoldering, more deadly stage of a white-hot wrath. Those who did not know him had often mistaken the agreeable tone he was using now as friendly. Aly knew better.

"That was a stroke of genius if ever I saw it."

"That's one way of putting it," she said, beginning to get puzzled. Her father had given a hearty chuckle. This was a new touch.

"It was a hair-raising gamble, Aly, but I won't scold." Lorne chuckled again. "I'd have done the same thing."

In the short silence Aly struggled to make sense of his words. Something was askew here. "And just how did I gamble?" she asked, her voice neutral.

"Oh, come on now, Alyson. You couldn't have been one hundred percent sure that Marshall would vote your proxy in favor of the board. You couldn't have been that positive of his love for you!"

Aly stood up, pinching off an exclamation just in time. She battled to keep her voice steady. "How—er—exactly how did it happen, Dad?"

"Well, about five minutes before the meeting Marshall strolled in with your proxy letter. I nearly had heart failure when I read it, Aly. Naturally he kept us all in the dark until the vote was taken for retaining the board. You know what we were expecting. I can't begin to describe to you my feelings when Marshall's hand went up in our favor. I don't think I've ever known such a feeling. I doubt I ever will again..." He cleared his throat.

Aly, her legs weak now, sat back down. "He had us, you know," Lorne said softly. "He had us, Aly. But you know that I could never even begin to imagine Marshall's...regard for you. I'm proud of you, Alyson. I'm proud of both of you."

"Thank you, Dad," she whispered.

"Bring Marshall around Thursday night for dinner. I'd like to know that young man better, and since he's apparently about to become a member of this family, it's time we put aside our differences. Frankly," he laughed shortly, "I'm relieved he's to become my son-in-law. Your brother needs all the help he can get in running this bank."

"I'll...ask him about Thursday," said Aly quietly. Through the oval glass, she could see a white Lincoln Continental approaching the house.

Walking to the door, she saw Marshall alight, the sun catching the sheen of his well-groomed head. Had he voted in favor of the board because he loved her or because, when push came to shove, he could not be less than Sy and Elizabeth's boy? She could not be sure. Examining his taut expression through the glass, she saw nothing to indicate her father's assumption was correct.

The suspense widened like an aching chasm inside her. Her breath came short and fast as she opened the door. Marshall reached back inside the car for something he slipped into his coat pocket.

Seeing her, he straightened and there was a moment of measuring silence before Marshall spoke. "I was hoping I'd find you here."

"Were you?" Aly asked noncommittally.

"I've just come from the stockholders' meeting."

"I know. My father just called."

"Then he told you how I voted your letter of proxy."

"He told me."

Approaching the porch, his gaze steady as hers, Marshall said, "I'm assuming the reason for that magnanimous gesture was to clear the books once and for all of any debts you somehow felt still outstanding between the Waynes and the Kingstons."

Aly remained silent. There was time enough for explanations later—if there was a later and if explanations were necessary.

"Or was it because, once you discovered why I was back in Claiborne, you thought I richly deserved the stock I'd schemed to get?" Marshall asked ironically as he propped a foot on the bottom step.

"Why did you vote in favor of the board, Marshall?"

"Don't you know why, Aly? Because I love you. Your proxy gave me the chance to prove that it's you I want and not your father's bank."

Aly put out a hand involuntarily, reeling from the shock of joy coursing through her. "Marshall—You love me? Why didn't you tell me before—"

"Aly, honey, don't you understand?" Taking the steps two at a time, he reached her and drew her into his arms where he rocked her gently, soothingly, like a child. "If I'd told you how I felt about you, that I want to spend the rest of my life trying to make you happy, you'd have just been more hurt when you found out the truth about why I'd come back to Claiborne. Nothing would have convinced you of my sincerity. You would have thought all I'd said had been a lie for the purpose of weaseling your stock out of you. I knew you'd toss me out on my ear once you'd learned why I was back. By not promising you anything, at least I could spare you something…"

Aly had begun to cry quietly from relief and emotional exhaustion. She felt weak all over and had to fight from sagging against him. "I feel limp as a rag," she muttered against the silk of his tie.

"You ought to," he said above her head. "It's taken a long time and a lot out of you to reel this boy in."

Aly looked up, grinning through her tears. "Have I done that?"

"Without a doubt. Look inside my coat pocket."

Aly felt in his pocket and drew out an old brown velvet ring box, very faded and worn. "Open it," Marshall said softly.

In the space between them, still in the circle of his arms, Aly lifted the lid. Inside, wedged in the ring groove, was a narrow band of gold. Aly looked up in flushed wonder, her throat tightening with emotion. "Elizabeth's ring!" she breathed.

"She always said a special girl waited for me, one who would want that ring around her finger. She was right, as usual—about the special girl, I mean. I sure am hoping she was right about the rest."

"Marshall," Aly said, her eyes luminous, her heart about to burst, "how can you have the least doubt?"

"Well," he said, tilting her chin, "there's a way to put to rest any doubts I may have."

As she closed her eyes, waiting for Marshall's lips to descend, Aly was conscious of the moment as both a conclusion and a beginning, the joining of two ends of time in a never-ending revolution, like the ring she would soon wear on her finger. They had been brought a full cycle, she realized. Everything had changed and yet all seemed the same as the day she first set foot on Cedar Hill. Wrens still chirped in the pecan trees, geraniums bobbed in clay pots, and the swing still creaked in the noonday breeze—a curious blend of the past and present, of time passing and standing still. And they were still here, too, she and Marshall, their hearts united at last.

Aly sighed against him, her arms tightening around his waist in loving possession. Marshall responded likewise. Out in the pasture, the russet stallion Sampson lifted his head, scenting the wind. He gave a glad whinney. His master was home.

Prologue

From a chair beside her bed, Leon Holloway leaned in close to his wife's wan face. She lay exhausted under clean sheets, eyes tightly closed, her hair brushed and face washed after nine harrowing hours of giving birth.

"Millicent, do you want to see the twins now? They need to be nursed," Leon said softly, stroking his wife's forehead.

"Only one," she said without opening her eyes. "Bring me only one. I couldn't abide two. You choose. Let the midwife take the other and give it to that do-gooder doctor of hers. He'll find it a good home."

"Millicent—" Leon drew back sharply. "You can't mean that."

"I do, Leon. I can bear the curse of one, but not two. Do what I say, or so help me, I'll drown them both."

"Millicent, honey... it's too early. You'll change your mind."

"Do what I say, Leon. I mean it."

Leon rose heavily. His wife's eyes were still closed, her lips tightly sealed. She had the bitterness in her to do as she threatened, he knew. He left the bedroom to go downstairs to the kitchen where the midwife had cleaned and wrapped the crying twins.

"They need to be fed," she said, her tone accusatory. "The

idea of a new mother wanting to get herself cleaned up before tending to the stomachs of her babies! I never heard of such a thing. I've a mind to put 'em to my own nipples, Mr. Holloway, if you'd take no offense at it. Lord knows I've got plenty of milk to spare."

"No offense taken, Mrs. Mahoney," Leon said, "and...I'd be obliged if you *would* wet-nurse one of them. My wife says she can feed only one mouth."

Mrs. Mahoney's face tightened with contempt. She was of Irish descent and her full, lactating breasts spoke of the recent delivery of her third child. She did not like the haughty, reddish-gold-haired woman upstairs who put such stock in her beauty. She would have liked to express to the missy's husband what she thought of his wife's cold, heartless attitude toward the birth of her newborns, unexpected though the second one was, but the concern of the moment was the feeding of the child. She began to unbutton the bodice of her dress. "I will, Mr. Holloway. Which one?"

Leon squeezed shut his eyes and turned his back to her. He could not bear to look upon the tragedy of choosing which twin to feast at the breast of its mother while allocating the other to the milk of a stranger. "Rearrange their order or leave them the same," he ordered the midwife. "I'll point to the one you're to take."

He heard the midwife follow his instructions, then pointed a finger over his shoulder. When he turned around again, he saw that the one taken was the last born, the one for whom he'd hurriedly found a holey sheet to serve as a bed and covering. Quickly, Leon scooped up the infant left. His sister was already suckling hungrily at her first meal. "I'll be back, Mrs. Mahoney. Please don't leave. You and I must talk."

Chapter One

On the day Nathan Holloway's life changed forever, his morning began like any other. Zak, the German shepherd he'd rescued and raised from a pup, licked a warm tongue over his face. Nathan wiped at the wet wake-up call and pushed him away. "Aw, Zak," he said, but in a whisper so as not to awaken his younger brother, sleeping in his own bed across the room. Sunrise was still an hour away, and the room was dark and cold. Nathan shivered in his night shift. He had left his underwear, shirt, and trousers on a nearby chair for quiet and easy slipping into as he did every night before climbing into bed. Randolph still had another hour's sleep coming to him, and there would be hell to pay if Nathan disturbed his brother.

Socks and boots in hand and with the dog following, Nathan let himself out into the hall and sat on a bench to pull them on. The smell of bacon and onions frying drifted up from the kitchen. Nothing better for breakfast than bacon and onions on a cold morning with a day of work ahead, Nathan thought. Zak, attentive to his master's every move and thought, wagged his tail in agreement. Nathan chuckled softly and gave the animal's neck a quick, rough rub. There would be potatoes and hot biscuits with butter and jam, too.

His mother was at the stove, turning bacon. She was already dressed, hair in its neat bun, a fresh apron around her trim form. "G'morning, Mother," Nathan said sleepily, passing by her to hurry outdoors to the privy. Except for his sister, the princess, even in winter, the menfolks were discouraged from using the chamber pot in the morning. They had to head to the outhouse. Afterward, Nathan would wash in the mudroom off the kitchen where it was warm and the water was still hot in the pitcher.

"Did you wake your brother?" his mother said without turning around.

"No, ma'am. He's still sleeping."

"He's got that big test today. You better not have awakened him."

"No, ma'am. Dad about?"

"He's seeing to more firewood."

As Nathan quickly buttoned into his jacket, his father came into the back door with an armload of the sawtooth oak they'd cut and stacked high in the fall. "Mornin', son. Sleep all right?"

"Yessir."

"Good boy. Full day ahead."

"Yessir."

It was their usual exchange. All days were full since Nathan had completed his schooling two years ago. A Saturday of chores awaited him every weekday, not that he minded. He liked farmwork, being outside, alone most days, just him and the sky and the land and the animals. Nathan took the lit lantern his father handed him and picked up a much-washed flour sack containing a milk bucket and towel. Zak followed him to the outhouse and did his business in the dark perimeter of the woods while Nathan did his, then Nathan and the dog went to the barn to attend to his before-breakfast chores, the light from the lantern leading the way.

Daisy, the cow, mooed an agitated greeting from her stall. "Hey, old girl," Nathan said. "We'll have you taken care of in a minute." Before grabbing a stool and opening the stall gate, Nathan shone the light around the barn to make sure no unwanted visitor had taken shelter during the cold March night. It was not unheard of to find a vagrant in the hayloft or, in warmer weather, to discover a snake curled in a corner. Once a hostile, wounded fox had taken refuge in the toolshed.

Satisfied that none had invaded, Nathan hung up the lantern and opened the stall gate. Daisy ambled out and went directly to her feed trough, where she would eat her breakfast while Nathan milked. He first brushed the cow's sides of hair and dirt that might fall into the milk, then removed the bucket from the sack and began to clean her teats with the towel. Finally he stuck the bucket under the cow's bulging udder, Zak sitting expectantly beside him, alert for the first squirt of warm milk to relieve the cow's discomfort.

Daisy allowed only Nathan to milk her. She refused to cooperate with any other member of the family. Nathan would press his hand to her right flank, and the cow would obligingly move her leg back for him to set to his task. With his father and siblings, she'd keep her feet planted, and one of them would have to force her leg back while she bawled and trembled and waggled her head, no matter that her udder was being emptied. "You alone got the touch," his father would say to him.

That was all right by Nathan and with his brother and sister as well, two and three years behind him, respectively. They got to sleep later and did not have to hike to the barn in inclement weather before the sun was up, but Nathan liked this time alone. The scents of hay and the warmth of the animals, especially in winter, set him at ease for the day.

The milk collected, Nathan put the lid on the bucket and set it high out of Zak's reach while he fed and watered the horses and led the cow to the pasture gate to turn her out for grazing. The sun was rising, casting a golden glow over the brown acres of the Barrows homestead that would soon be awash with the first growth of spring wheat. It was still referred to as the Barrows farm, named for the line of men to whom it had been handed down since 1840. Liam Barrows, his mother's father, was the last heir to bear the name. Liam's two sons had died before they could inherit, and the land had gone to his daughter, Millicent Holloway. Nathan was aware that someday the place would belong to him. His younger brother, Randolph, was destined for bigger and better things, he being the smarter, and his sister, Lily, would marry, she being beautiful and already sought after by sons of the well-to-do in Gainesville and Montague and Denton, even from towns across the border in the Indian Territory. "I won't be living out my life in a calico dress and kitchen apron" was a statement the family often heard from his sister, the princess.

That was all fine by Nathan, too. He got along well with his siblings, but he was not one of them. His brother and sister were close, almost like twins. They had the same dreams—to be rich and become somebody—and were focused on the same goal: to get off the farm. At nearly twenty, Nathan had already decided that to be rich was to be happy where you were, doing the things you liked, and wanting for nothing more.

So it was that that morning, when he left the barn with milk bucket in hand, his thoughts were on nothing more than the hot onions and bacon and buttered biscuits that awaited him before

he set out to repair the fence in the south pasture after breakfast. His family was already taking their seats at the table when
he entered the kitchen. Like always, his siblings took chairs that
flanked his mother's place at one end of the table while he seated
himself next to his father's at the other. The family arrangement
had been such as long as Nathan could remember: Randolph
and Lily and his mother in one group, he and his father in another. Like a lot of things, it was something he'd been aware of
but never noticed until the stranger appeared in the late afternoon.

Chapter Two

The sun was behind him and sinking fast when Nathan stowed hammer and saw and nails and started homeward, carrying his toolbox and lunch pail. The sandwiches his mother had prepared with the extra bacon and onions and packed in the pail with pickles, tomato, and boiled egg had long disappeared, and he was hungry for his supper. It would be waiting when he returned, but it would be a while before he sat down to the evening meal. He had Daisy to milk. His siblings would have fed the horses and pigs and chickens before sundown, so he'd have only the cow to tend before he washed up and joined the family at the table.

It was always something he looked forward to, going home at the end of the day. His mother was a fine cook and served rib-sticking fare, and he enjoyed the conversation round the table and the company of his family before going to bed. Soon, his siblings would be gone. Randolph, a high school senior, seventeen, had already been accepted at Columbia University in New York City to begin his studies, aiming for law school after college. His sister, sixteen, would no doubt be married within a year or two. How the evenings would trip along when they were gone, he didn't know. Nathan didn't contribute much to the gatherings. Like his father, his thoughts on things were seldom asked and almost never offered. He was merely a quiet listener, a fourth at cards and board games (his mother did not play), and a dependable source to bring in extra wood, stoke the fire, and replenish cups of cocoa. Still, he felt a part of the family scene if for the most part ignored, like the indispensable clock over the mantel in the kitchen.

Zak trotted alongside him unless distracted by a covey of doves to flush, a rabbit to chase. Nathan drew in a deep breath of the cold late-March air, never fresher than at dusk when the day had lost its sun and the wind had subsided, and expelled it with a sense of satisfaction. He'd had a productive day. His father would be pleased that he'd been able to repair the whole south fence and that the expense of extra lumber had been justified. Sometimes they disagreed on what needed to be done for the amount of the expenditure, but his father always listened to his son's judgment and often let him have his way. More times than not, Nathan had heard his father say to his mother, "The boy's got a head for what's essential for the outlay, that's for sure." His mother rarely answered unless it was to give a little sniff or utter a *humph*, but Nathan understood her reticence was to prevent him from getting a big head.

As if his head would ever swell over anything, he thought, especially when compared to his brother and sister. Nathan considered that everything about him—when he considered himself at all—was as ordinary as a loaf of bread. Except for his height and strong build and odd shade of blue-green eyes, nothing about him was of any remarkable notice. Sometimes, a little ruefully, he thought that when it came to him, he'd stood somewhere in the middle of the line when the good Lord passed out exceptional intellects, talent and abilities, personalities, and looks while Randolph and Lily had been at the head of it. He accepted his lot without rancor, for what good was a handsome face and winning personality for growing wheat and running a farm?

Nathan was a good thirty yards from the first outbuildings before he noticed a coach and team of two horses tied to the hitching post in front of the white wood-framed house of his home. He could not place the pair of handsome Thoroughbreds and expensive Concord. No one that he knew in Gainesville owned horses and carriage of such distinction. He guessed the owner was a rich new suitor of Lily's who'd ridden up from Denton or from Montague across the county line. She'd met several such swains a couple of months ago when the wealthiest woman in town, his mother's godmother, had hosted a little coming-out party for his sister. Nathan puzzled why he'd shown up to court her during the school week at this late hour of the day. His father wouldn't like that, not that he'd have much say in it. When it came to his sister, his mother had the last word, and she encouraged Lily's rich suitors.

Nathan had turned toward the barn when a head appeared above a window of the coach. It belonged to a middle-aged man who, upon seeing Nathan, quickly opened the door and hopped out. "I say there, me young man!" he called to Nathan. "Are ye the lad we've come to see?"

An Irishman, sure enough, and obviously the driver of the carriage, Nathan thought. He automatically glanced behind him as though half expecting the man to have addressed someone else. Turning back his gaze, he called, "Me?"

"Yes, you."

"I'm sure not."

"If ye are, ye'd best go inside. He doesn't like to be kept waiting."

"Who doesn't like to be kept waiting?"

"Me employer, Mr. Trevor Waverling."

"Never heard of him." Nathan headed for the barn.

"Wait! Wait!" the man cried, scrambling after him. "Ye must go inside, lad. Mr. Waverling won't leave until ye do." The driver had caught up with Nathan. "I'm cold and…me back-side's shakin' hands with me belly. I ain't eaten since breakfast," he whined.

Despite the man's desperation and his natty cutaway coat, striped trousers, and stiff top hat befitting the driver of such a distinctive conveyance, Nathan thought him comical. He was not of particularly short stature, but his legs were not long enough for the rest of him. His rotund stomach seemed to rest on their trunks, no space between, and his ears and Irish red hair stuck out widely beneath the hat like a platform for a stovepipe. He reminded Nathan of a circus clown he'd once seen.

"Well, that's too bad," Nathan said. "I've got to milk the cow." He hurried on, curious of who Mr. Waverling was and the reason he wished to see him. If so, his father would have sent his farmhand to get him, and he must tend to Daisy.

The driver ran back to the house and Nathan hurried to the barn. Before he reached it, he heard Randolph giving Daisy a smack. "Stay still, damn you!"

"What are you doing?" Nathan exclaimed from the open door, surprised to see Randolph and Lily attempting to milk Daisy.

"What does it look like?" Randolph snapped.

"Get away from her," Nathan ordered. "That's my job."

"Let him do it," Lily pleaded. "I can't keep holding her leg back."

"We can't," Randolph said. "Dad said to send him to the house the minute he showed up."

203

His siblings often discussed him in the third person in his presence. Playing cards and board games, they'd talk about him as if he weren't sitting across the table from them. "Wonder what card he has," they'd say to each other. "Do you suppose he'll get my king?"

"Both of you get away from her," Nathan commanded. "I'm not going anywhere until I milk Daisy. Easy, old girl," he said, running a hand over the cow's quivering flanks. "Nathan is here."

Daisy let out a long bawl, and his brother and sister backed away. When it came to farm matters, after their father, Nathan had the top say.

"Who is Mr. Waverling, and why does he want to see me?" Nathan asked.

Brother and sister looked at each other. "We don't know," they both piped together, Lily adding, "But he's rich."

"We were sent out of the house when the man showed up," Randolph said, "but Mother and Dad and the man are having a shouting match over you."

"Me?" Nathan pulled Daisy's teats, taken aback. Who would have a shouting match over him? "That's all you know?" he asked. Zak had come to take his position at his knee and was rewarded with a long arc of milk into his mouth.

"That's all we know, but we think...we think he's come to take you away, Nathan," Lily said. Small, dainty, she came behind her older brother and put her arms around him, leaning into his back protectively. "I'm worried," she said in a small voice.

"Me, too," Randolph chimed in. "Are you in trouble? You haven't done anything bad, have you, Nathan?"

"Not that I know of," Nathan said. Take him away? What was this?

"What a silly thing to ask, Randolph," Lily scolded. "Nathan never does anything bad."

"I know that, but I had to ask," her brother said. "It's just that the man is important. Mother nearly collapsed when she saw him. Daddy took charge and sent us out of the house immediately. Do you have any idea who he is?"

"None," Nathan said, puzzled. "Why should I?"

"I don't know. He seemed to know about you. And you look like him...a little."

Another presence had entered the barn. They all turned to see their father standing in the doorway. He cleared his throat. "Nathan," he said, his voice heavy with sadness, "when the milkin's done, you better come to the house. Randolph, you and Lily stay here."

"But I have homework," Randolph protested.

"It can wait," Leon said as he turned to go. "Drink the milk for your supper."

The milking completed and Daisy back in her stall, Nathan left the barn, followed by the anxious gazes of his brother and sister. Dusk had completely fallen, cold and biting. His father had stopped halfway to the house to wait for him. Nathan noticed the circus clown had scrambled back into the carriage. "What's going on, Dad?" he said.

His father suddenly bent forward and pressed his hands to his face.

"Dad! What in blazes—?" Was his father crying? "What's the matter? What's happened?"

A tall figure stepped out of the house onto the porch. He paused, then came down the steps toward them, the light from the house at his back. He was richly dressed in an overcoat of fine wool and carried himself with an air of authority. He was a handsome man in a lean, wolfish sort of way, in his forties, Nathan guessed. "I am what's happened," he said.

Nathan looked him up and down. "Who are you?" he demanded, the question bored into the man's sea-green eyes, so like his own. He would not have dared, but he wanted to put his arm protectively around his father's bent shoulders.

"I am your father," the man said.

About the Author

Leila Meacham is a writer and former teacher who lives in San Antonio, Texas. She is the bestselling author of the novels *Roses*, *Tumbleweeds*, *Somerset*, *Titans*, and *Ryan's Hand*. For more information, you can visit LeilaMeacham.com.

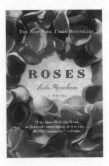

"Heralded as the new *Gone with the Wind*" (*USA Today*), this acclaimed novel brings back the epic storytelling that readers have always loved—in a panoramic saga of dreams, power struggles, and forbidden passions in East Texas…

The epic storytelling of *Roses* meets the moving drama of *Friday Night Lights* in this heartrending story of three friends who forge a lifelong bond against the backdrop of a Texas town's passion for football.

Gone with the Wind meets *The Help* in the stunning prequel to Leila Meacham's *New York Times* bestselling family epic, *Roses*.

A sweeping new drama of long-hidden secrets, enduring bonds, and redemption set in turn-of-the-century Texas.

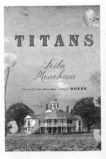